The firefighter pulled out and handed her the container.

"Here, get a few swallows of water. You've inhaled a lot of smoke." A strand of his blond hair fell out from under his helmet. Clean shaven, with high cheekbones. His blue-green eyes reminded her of a glassy sea, kind and understanding.

Her stare went beyond his broad shoulders to the burning forest fire in the distance.

"Do you know what happened?" His eyebrows narrowed.

"I was vacationing alone until three prison escapees broke in and tied me up. One of them was my cousin," she mumbled.

He offered his hand. "How did they know where to find you? Do you know where they went?" His eyes searched her. "Think you can walk? We need to get beyond that fire line before the blaze spreads. My team is over there waiting to get you out of here."

"I think so." She squeezed his hand, and he helped her up. Her nose met with his chin in height. "I'm a little dizzy, but I can walk."

"Lean on me." He looped his arm around her waist and carried a strange tool in his other hand.

After the events of the last few days, she was badly in need of a rescue. Her thoughts were scrambled, her head hurt and the frown on his face told her he suspected she'd helped the prisoners escape. How far could she trust Kendall Simpson? Would he believe her if she tried to explain?

Loretta Eidson is an award-winning author born and raised in the South. Her debut novel, *Pursued in the Wilderness*, released September 2022. Her love of reading began at a young age after she discovered Phyllis A. Whitney's mystery novels. Loretta believes in the power of prayer and loves the motto "God will make a way where there appears to be no way." She lives in North Mississippi and enjoys time with her family. Visit Loretta on her website at lorettaeidson.com.

Books by Loretta Eidson

Love Inspired Mountain Rescue

Pursued in the Wilderness

Visit the Author Profile page at LoveInspired.com.

Blue Ridge Mountain Escape

LORETTA EIDSON

LOVE INSPIRED
INSPIRATIONAL ROMANCE

LOVE INSPIRED®
INSPIRATIONAL ROMANCE

Recycling programs for this product may not exist in your area.

ISBN-13: 978-1-335-46837-6

Blue Ridge Mountain Escape

Copyright © 2023 by Loretta Eidson

For questions and comments about the quality of this book, please contact us at CustomerService@Harlequin.com.

Love Inspired
22 Adelaide St. West, 41st Floor
Toronto, Ontario M5H 4E3, Canada
www.LoveInspired.com

Printed in U.S.A.

Be strong and of a good courage, fear not, nor be afraid of them: for the Lord thy God, he it is that doth go with thee; he will not fail thee, nor forsake thee.

—*Deuteronomy* 31:6

I dedicate this book to all forest service firefighters who freely give themselves to preserving and protecting nature, wildlife, human lives and property in our national parks, plus all firefighters across the country, including my firefighter/EMT son, Carey, and my EMS battalion chief son-in-law, Jason.

Chapter One

This had been the worst few days of Haley Gordon's life.

Her boyfriend had been lying to her all along. How had she missed the signs with the constant gifts and undivided attention every time he returned from his so-called business trips? She fumed and blinked away tears. Should've known their relationship was too good to be true. Thoughts of his deceit sent heat to her cheeks.

Then, if that wasn't bad enough, her best friend, whom she always confided in, got sick two days ago and bailed on their vacation in the Blue Ridge Mountains of North Carolina, which made it too late to cancel the trip. She decided to go anyway.

Now the curvy drive up the mountain surrounded her with the colors of fall. Red, yellow, orange and green blends of the leaves shaded the two-lane road. A beautiful canvas of God's creation and the perfect place for her to rest and find peace in her chaotic life. She was admiring how beautiful everything was until she was jolted back to reality by a call on her satellite phone.

"Hey, Mom, I just turned off the main highway. It's beautiful out here. How'd Dad's appointment go with the doctor this morning?"

"The cardiologist moved your dad's surgery up to next Friday," her mom said. "But I don't want to mess up your vacation."

Haley bit her lip. "You're not messing up my vacation. You know I'll be there." She brushed her fingers through her hair with one hand. She desperately needed some downtime. "I love you. I'll see you later in the week."

She swallowed the lump forming in her throat and pushed back her disappointment. A deer pranced across the narrow pavement in front of her. Her foot slammed on the brake. She screamed at the near miss. "Whoa. That was close."

The late afternoon sun cast shadows through the trees. Haley continued her journey, driving slower while keeping a keen eye out for more deer. A small wooden sign pointed to her assigned two-bedroom rental cabin surrounded by tall pine trees.

A nagging thought surfaced. This area was close to the prison where her cousin Blake was incarcerated. She didn't want to think about any more negative things, or something that might help lead into it. She pushed the thought away, turned and parked close to the front door. Then stepped out of her car onto a thick layer of fallen pine needles and took in a deep breath of pine-scented mountain air. "I'm finally here."

A log bench sat on the small covered porch with a statue of a black bear beside it and a pinecone-and-grape-vine "Welcome" wreath hung on the front door. Such an inviting sight. Inside, the decor matched her expectations. Rustic, but nice. A couch and chair made of logs with green-leaf-patterned, thick cushions that almost matched the curtains. The lamps on the end tables appeared to have been made from deer antlers. Everything looked woodsy. A pleasant change from her contemporary decor in her apartment in the city.

Haley meandered across the creaking floor into the kitchen and ran her fingers across the dark green countertop. She smiled at all the bear-shaped kitchen accessories. Salt-and-pepper shakers on the round wood dining table, canisters, and a paper towel holder next to the sink. Too cute. The resort went all out to create a forest wildlife setting.

Her bedroom matched the rest of the furniture with a thick log headboard and matching chest of drawers. Too bad her friend would miss out on the experience.

She unloaded her suitcase and a box of supplies before darkness draped over the forest. Crickets chirped and frogs croaked while she organized her snacks and refrigerator goods in the kitchen, then unpacked her suitcase in the chest and set her small travel alarm clock on the nightstand, noting the late hour, 8:43 p.m. Weary from her day, she made herself a sandwich and turned in early. So peaceful. Her body sank into the soft mattress. She closed her eyes as the sounds of crickets chirping and the hoot of an owl lulled her to sleep.

Voices. Was she dreaming?

Her eyes popped open. Loud male voices seeped into her bedroom through the log walls. What time was it? Her clock read 1:35 a.m. Why was their cabin so close to hers? The creaking of their footsteps sounded like they were in the same cabin as her, and the delicious aroma of steaks cooking on a grill made her mouth water. Frustration assaulted her desire for a good night's rest. She tossed in bed, covered her head with a pillow.

"Why me? Why does everything seem to be falling apart? I can't get a break." Tears spilled out and dampened the pillowcase. Her seven-day getaway was supposed to be quiet and calming. Unlike the rest of her life. In the midst of all the drama with her boyfriend, she had lost her job as a dental assistant. What decent company puts a *No Longer in Business* sign on the door and doesn't inform staff first?

Too bad she no longer had a boyfriend, a trustworthy one. He could've rented the cabin next door and she wouldn't have this problem with neighbors. They could've enjoyed cooking out and hiking trails together. But no, she'd overheard him talking on his cell. He'd expressed his love and said to give the kids a hug for him.

She'd confronted him and he finally admitted his weekend work trips were to visit his wife and kids.

How infuriating. How could he do that to her? Betrayal and lies cut deep, not to mention the humiliation and embarrassment of not knowing she'd been dating a married man.

If she ever dated again, the guy would have to prove himself trustworthy before she'd consider him a friend or a boyfriend. She'd check his ring finger for a tan line or for an indention in the skin, and she certainly wouldn't fall prey to his deception. She'd been duped once and wouldn't put herself in that situation again.

Haley punched her pillow and flipped onto her back. Would her mind ever shut down and let her rest? Her mom's voice reverberated in her thoughts. *The cardiologist moved your dad's surgery up to next Friday.* Meaning she'd have to leave Thursday in time to drive home, unpack and be ready to sit with her mom in the hospital waiting room. Not that she minded. She didn't, but the timing couldn't have been worse.

What else could go wrong?

She yawned. Why did it still feel like those men were in her cabin? Sound must travel in the forest. Tomorrow she'd request a cabin far away from her noisy neighbors. She sighed and willed herself to forget all the negatives in her life and go to sleep. Tomorrow would be a new day.

Another creak too close to ignore.

Her eyes popped open and fear sent goose bumps skittering all over her body.

Someone's in my room.

She slid her sweaty palms out from under the cover as she lay in the pitch black. Her breath stalled. She listened intently for movement. Only the sounds of crickets and the hoot of an owl filled the silence. Another creak closer. A pungent stench hit her nostrils. Body odor? Her breath released and came out in short huffs. Would she hyperventilate? She bolted upright. A large hand covered her mouth, muffling her scream. His hand smelled of nicotine.

She grabbed at the brawny arm and kicked the cover off. The ceiling light came on, illuminating three men in prison-orange jumpsuits. Adrenaline shot her pulse into overtime. One lanky man with dark, deep-set eyes leaned against the doorframe. He popped open a can of soda with a smirky grin on his face. Her focus landed on the face of the sandy-haired man covering her mouth.

She stilled and blinked to make sure she saw correctly. Her heart pounded against her chest and her breath hitched. Her cousin Blake? He was supposed to be in prison for aggravated assault with a deadly weapon. What was he doing here? How had he found her, and who was the tattooed muscle man standing behind him?

"I'll take my hand away if you promise not to scream." The glare in Blake's narrowed blue-green eyes and his tight lips told her he meant business. He eased his hand away, and she scrambled to a sitting position on the side of the bed.

"What have you done, Blake? How did you get out of prison?" She glanced at the convicts staring back at her. "How did you find me?" She never expected to see him again, nor this crude side of him. He'd respected her in the past, or so she thought. She couldn't help that his dad drank too much and slapped him around. He'd confided in her throughout their childhood and most of their teen years. They'd been the best of friends until he met up with the wrong crowd and grew distant.

"Do as you're told, and you won't get hurt." Blake cocked his head sideways and popped his neck, a quirk she'd seen him do many times as a teenager. "Mac, Connor and I appreciate you lettin' us hide out here until our friend brings us some clothes."

"How'd you get out? Did you kill somebody?" She pressed her lips together and fumed. "I don't want any part of your prison break. Get what you want and leave."

"Gutsy, isn't she? Get on with it, Blake. Time's wasting," Mac said. Not only were his arms decorated with colorful tattoos, but he had a scar across his cheek and he chewed on a twig. His deep set, cold eyes and sneering expression were threatening enough.

"Like it or not, you're already involved." Blake grabbed her arm and hauled her out of bed. "It's none of your business how we escaped. But if you must know, we had help from a reliable source on the inside. And no, we haven't killed anyone yet."

Yet. Did that mean they planned to kill me? Apprehension of their unknown intent twisted in her gut. *Lord, I don't want to die.*

Haley's bare feet landed on the cool floor. She'd opted to sleep in warm navy lounge pants and a light blue color coordinated long-sleeved T-shirt. Standing before these three rough-looking men, at least she'd covered her body.

"But how did you find me?" She tugged her arm from Blake's grip.

"Easy. We broke into the main office for a map of the mountain and empty cabins. The registry was laying open." He turned her toward the bedroom door. "I spotted your name and cabin number. It showed you were the only person occupying the place. Who would have thought our escape would work out so perfect and we'd find you here? I figured you'd be happy to see me."

"Not under these circumstances, and certainly not with your friends." She pursed her lips. "You should have found an empty cabin."

"That's enough talk. Make us some coffee." Mac's gruff voice sent a shiver through her. He showed his pistol and followed her into the kitchen.

Was he trying to intimidate her? It worked. She straightened and held her head high in hopes of not appearing afraid.

"There weren't any empty cabins. If I hadn't spotted your name, someone else would be making coffee for us right now." Blake followed her through the bedroom door. "We only want a place to hole up until our friend joins us with street clothes, then we'll be on our way. You wouldn't want your favorite cousin to sleep in the wild, now, would you?"

"Yes. I'm sure you've had it worse, and you lived through it." She took her time walking to the kitchen so she could calculate an escape route. The probability of running looked slim. She picked up the black bear coffee canister and scooped coffee grounds into the filter of the drip coffeepot. The delight of seeing all the black bear accessories lost its appeal. Would Blake let these guys harm her or shoot her? Would they let her live, knowing she could alert the authorities?

Blake's scowl and suspecting eyes followed her every move. He glanced out the window, then back at her. The tall guy named Connor sat in the living room chair with one leg hiked over the arm. Nonchalant and relaxed, like he had nothing to worry about. Mac leaned against the refrigerator, still chewing the end of a twig. His stare made her shudder. Who was the fourth person they mentioned? A spouse, friend—or another escapee?

The coffeepot gurgled its last drops into the pot. She poured the fresh brew into square-shaped ceramic mugs and set them on the kitchen table. Blake removed the tiebacks from the window curtains and walked toward her. Her mouth went dry. Was he going to strangle her?

I don't want to die.

His hard-core grimace unnerved her even more. She missed his lighthearted personality. They used to climb trees together and run the open pasture on their grandparents' farm. He'd been fun and adventurous, always filled with pranks that made her laugh. This was a side of him she'd never seen. Probably caused by his dad's badgering and telling him he'd never amount to anything. Of course, he *was* an adult and had the option to make better decisions.

He turned her around and tied her hands behind her back so tight she thought he'd cut off the circulation. Mac jerked drawers open in the kitchen until he found duct tape. He tore a strip off and pressed it over her mouth. Her pulse raced.

"That will keep her quiet." Mac's hostile demeanor unnerved her. Not someone she wanted to anger.

There was no sense in fighting Blake with his six-two height. He'd grown taller than she remembered and was no match for Haley's five-seven. One of his punches would knock her out. He walked her to the bedroom and checked the window locks. "Stay quiet and you just might live to enjoy the rest of your vacation."

Some vacation.

"I'm sorry, Haley. I didn't want to involve you. But I knew you wouldn't want me, your favorite cousin, to live the rest of my life in prison." He turned out the light and paused at the door. "You know I'm not a bad guy. I only need a little time to get away. You'll help me, won't you? After all we've been through together?"

She bore a hole in him with her eyes, not that he could see her glaring. He walked out and closed the door. Darkness suffocated her. Sure, they'd had fun growing up together, but he was the one who became hostile and angry, and parted ways. All she knew to do was pray for him.

Haley inched back until her legs bumped into the mattress. She sat on the bed and hoped they'd leave or go to sleep. Even if they went to sleep, with all the creaks in the floor and her hands tied, she'd never make it past them to the front door and she couldn't reach the bedroom window locks.

She rested her head against the bed's log headboard. She *had* felt bad for Blake when he'd gone to prison. But no more. He'd destroyed any trust she'd ever had in him. Maybe if she did what he asked, he'd let her go. If she lived through this, one thing was for sure, between Blake and her ex-boyfriend, she'd never blindly give her trust to anyone again. And she'd never again travel alone.

The escapees laughed and talked for what seemed like hours. Their boisterous voices trailed through the wall and penetrated her ears. Something shattered. Her shoulders jerked at the sudden noise.

"You missed the sink, Connor." Blake chuckled. "Thought you played basketball."

"I'm out of practice. Want me to throw your cup?"

Mac interrupted the cup toss conversation and talked about all his plans for future extravagant vacations. Connor's scratchy voice expressed his desire to climb Mount Everest, while Blake wanted to settle down in a cabin hidden in the Rocky Mountains. They reminisced about how they succeeded in their escape.

Haley didn't want to hear any more. Uncertainty

of her safety had her in knots, and yet weariness crept over her. She willed herself to relax and closed her eyes.

Restless sleep assaulted her while nightmares of inhaling smoke, choking and running for her life mingled with voices and distant snoring. Her eyes opened as she coughed into the duct tape and sat up, sniffing the scent of wood burning and smoke. A hazy light filtered through the window. Morning hadn't come soon enough, but something wasn't right.

The smell of smoke wasn't coming from outside, but inside the cabin. And the muffled voices from her dream belonged to Blake and his friends. They were still here. Why hadn't they made a run for it already? She scooted from the bed until her feet touched the floor, then she edged over to where she'd left her rubber-soled house shoes by the dresser.

A sudden loud banging on the front door startled her. A man yelled, "Firefighter! Everyone needs to evacuate!" Scuffling noises came from the living room. Haley backed up to the bedroom door and twisted the doorknob with her tied hands, and opened the door. A cloud of smoke hung in the stifling air.

Blake and his friends fought with a man wearing a white hard hat. Two more firefighters ran inside. A bigger fight broke out in the smoke-filled room. She let out a muffled scream. Connor backed up, slinging his arms, and bumped into her. She plummeted to the floor and hit her head on the end table.

Rushing steps grew distant. The front door slammed shut; that had been her only escape route from the approaching fire. Blake had left her for dead. Had the firefighters seen her on the floor? Would anyone come back before it was too late?

Haley coughed into the duct tape and sucked in a deep, smoke-filled breath through her nostrils. It stung. Fresh air, she needed fresh air. She rolled to her side and tried to get up, but the room spun, and everything went dark.

Her ears rung. The door opened. Someone patted her cheeks and felt her pulse. Heavy footsteps clomped by her head. Who was there? Had Blake or Mac come back to kill her? A burning sensation filtered through her nose and into her lungs. She couldn't keep her eyes open and any efforts to cough choked her. Weakness settled in. Was she suffocating?

The footsteps returned and stopped beside her. She cringed and waited for the final blow. More pats to her cheeks forced her eyes open, but only for a moment. A man wearing a white hard hat and yellow shirt eased off the tape covering her mouth and untied her hands. She gasped for breath and coughed. Was she dreaming that this handsome man had scooped her into his powerful arms as though she weighed no more than a feather? His comforting voice announced he was a Forest Service firefighter. Haley's body bounced with his every step.

She sucked in the mountain air.

"That's it. Take some deep breaths. You've inhaled

a lot of smoke." Her hand touched the cool ground when he set her down and leaned her against a tree stump. Her eyes opened as she responded to his voice and inhaled more of the fresh yet smoke-scented air.

He lifted a handheld radio to his mouth. "Simpson here. Four men fought with us and ran into the forest. I have a female, approximately twenty-six years old. She's inhaled a lot of smoke. Found her tied up and gagged. Coming your way."

The radio squawked. "Make it quick. Not looking stable over here. Looks like a blowup forming."

He turned his head toward the forest, and she looked beyond him. Another firefighter assisted a man who limped by his side. From the neighboring cabin, maybe?

"I'm Kendall Simpson, by the way." He'd turned his focus back to her.

"Haley Gordon." She rubbed the back of her head and blinked her burning, watering eyes. "What's a blowup?" Her throat hurt and her voice came out a little raspy.

The firefighter dug into his oversize backpack and pulled out a large plastic bottle. He unscrewed the top and handed her the container.

"Here, get a few swallows of water." A strand of his blond hair fell out from under his helmet. Clean shaven, with high cheekbones. His blue-green eyes reminded her of a glassy sea, kind and understanding. "We've rescued your friend, too. He's already with my team. A blowup is a term we use when there's a sudden increase in fire intensity."

"What friend? And what about the people in the other cabin?" Her stare went beyond his broad shoulders to the burning forest fire in the distance. Had the men in the cabin gotten out before the fire reached them? Would Blake and his friends make it out of the forest with this blaze behind them?

"The man we found on the ground outside your door. Someone did a number on him. Do you know what happened?" His eyebrows narrowed.

"I don't know who you're talking about." She rubbed her throat and coughed. "There were some men in the cabin close by. Could be one of them. I was vacationing alone until three escapees broke in and tied me up." Her fuzzy thoughts struggled to figure out what had happened. "One of them was my cousin," she mumbled.

"Escapees?" He stood and frowned. Then he offered his hand. "How did they know where to find you? Do you know where they went?" His eyes searched her. "Think you can walk? We need to get beyond that fire line before the blaze spreads. My handcrew team is over there waiting to get you out of here."

"I think so." She squeezed his hand, and he helped her up. Her nose met with his chin in height. The forest swayed. "I'm a little dizzy, but I can walk."

"You can lean on me." He looped his arm around her waist and carried a strange tool in his other hand.

"What's that?" She let him help her walk.

"It's one of my firefighting tools. It's called a Pulaski." He moved it out in front of her. "Has an ax on one end and an adze on the other, like a cutting tool or a hoe."

She hadn't needed a lesson in tools, but she had asked. After the events of the last few days, she was badly in need of a rescue. Her thoughts were scrambled, her head hurt and the frown on his face told her he suspected she'd helped the prisoners escape. How far could she trust Kendall Simpson? Would he believe her if she tried to explain?

What is she not telling me?

Kendall held this light-brown-haired, brown-eyed lady around the waist and rushed toward his teammates as fast as he could. Her story didn't quite add up.

He looked around for suspicious movements. The escapees were out there somewhere. He'd heard a special bulletin on his truck radio this morning on the way to work about three convicts who escaped from Stantonville Prison with the aid of a guard during the night. Authorities alleged they'd head to the mountains and were armed and dangerous. Their assessment was correct. He'd seen them firsthand.

Kendall's thoughts mused. What if he had single-handedly captured the criminals? How amazing would that have been? His superiors would probably recognize him, and he might get that promotion he wanted. His dad might even come around and finally be proud of him after their dispute over him not going into the family welding business.

Didn't matter what his ex-girlfriend thought.

She'd left him after he'd been involved in an extremely risky situation doing his job. She'd known he was a firefighter but claimed she didn't want to live in fear of him dying in a fire. He refused to give up the job he loved to appease her. Guess that relationship wasn't meant to be. He had prayed the right girl would come along, only to feel those prayers had landed on deaf ears.

"Is that your white SUV back there?" Kendall prodded with curiosity. He'd spotted something orange in the passenger seat of the vehicle in front of her cabin and had inspected it briefly prior to entering. Three orange prison jumpsuits. He had shoved them in his already full backpack to give to the authorities.

Was she involved with their escape, and they didn't need her anymore? Why not shoot her rather than leave her to die of smoke inhalation? Too many questions swirled around in his head. Saving people was his calling. But something told him Haley wasn't like any of the other people he'd rescued. Her reaction to his question appeared to be an insult.

She stiffened and pushed away. "Oh no. My car. Yes, I need to move it."

His radio squawked again. "Simpson, look out. Tree falling."

A loud, familiar cracking caught his attention. He grabbed her arm. "Look out! Run now!"

He barely heard the words of his teammates coming from his radio. The roar of the fire drowned them out. Their arms waved through the air, warning him to get out of the way of the falling pine tree. He had to get Haley to safety. A surge of energy kicked in and he tugged her, almost lifting her from the tree's landing path and away from flying debris.

The tree swooshed down and landed with a loud boom, blocking him from his team. Fire embers flew into the air and the wind tossed them in different directions, igniting the pine-needle-covered ground. Flames jumped around her vehicle and raced toward them. Intense heat hit his face. He'd lost sight of his friends.

His heart thumped wildly. Survival mode kicked in. So much for single-handedly capturing the escaped convicts. He must focus on keeping Haley and himself alive.

She screamed. "What do we do now? I don't want to die." Her voice cracked.

"Stay with me. I'll get you out of here." He scanned the area in search of a way around the danger zone.

"Simpson, can you hear me?" His teammate's voice scratched through his radio.

"Can't make it around the fire. Searching for another escape route." His rapid pulse went with fighting wildfires. But this time weighed heavier than normal. One wrong decision, and things wouldn't end well for either of them.

Haley halted and rubbed her thighs. "Hold on. My legs are killing me."

Smoke boiled into the sky. He studied the angry red, yellow and blue blaze moving toward them faster than he liked. It had cut them off from his crew and engulfed everything in its path. He gripped her arm and pointed to a boulder where she could have a brief reprieve. With the fire less than a third of a football field away and closing in, they didn't have much time. She slid to the ground and covered her face with her hands.

The whoosh of fire engulfing more trees and undergrowth grew closer and closer. His nerves were on edge. They had to put distance between them and the blaze. Smoke continued to thicken. He tugged her to her feet.

"Can't wait any longer. We've got to go." He put the Pulaski in the loop on his fire pack, wrapped his arm around her waist and helped her run.

"Thank you for helping me. I'm totally out of my element." Her voice staggered as they ran.

"It's what I do. By the way, I pulled three orange prison jumpsuits from your car. Care to share how they got there?" He glanced in her direction while he evaluated their next move and realized his question had a more accusing tone than he'd intended.

Her expression shifted from fearful to what he interpreted as defensive. Her lips tightened and her eyes narrowed. "I had nothing to do with those jumpsuits. Three escapees broke into my cabin. They tied me up and gagged me, but you should know that. You found me. They left me there to die."

"Didn't know if you knew where they were headed." Although he hadn't prayed in a while, he wondered if God intervened and sent them in the opposite direction.

"All I know is someone was bringing them a change of clothes. I wasn't privy to any more information." She wiped her forehead. "They had handguns, too."

Even more reason he didn't want to run into them again. The boulder hadn't shielded them for long. The wind had changed direction. Their only escape was uphill, which was not recommended. Fire climbs about as fast as a white-tailed deer could run. He bit his lip. This was not how he expected his day would go.

He helped her over an old log and noted for the first time she wore house shoes. No wonder she wasn't getting much traction through the forest. Didn't matter now. They'd have to make the best of it.

"I heard a special bulletin on my radio this morning describing them as armed and dangerous." Kendall wanted to believe her, but it didn't make sense the escapees would take a chance of letting her live if she could identify them, especially her cousin. He reached for her hand. "We've got to keep moving."

"I'd say their report is accurate." She took her hand away and followed close behind him. "I get the impression you think I had something to do with their escape."

"I can't be the judge. My responsibility is to get you out of here unscathed, and I intend to do just that." He took long strides, climbing the upgrade.

How long would she last? Her huffing proved her lack of mountain climbing experience.

"Think what you want. I can't keep up with your fast pace." She stopped, leaned over with her hands on her knees and blew out deep breaths. "My head is pounding."

Kendall returned to her side. "Breathe in and out slowly and try to relax. We have no choice but to keep going." Perspiration rolled down the sides of his face. He wiped it away with the sleeve of his shirt. He couldn't help but admire her tenacity to keep moving, even though she was out of breath and didn't have proper mountain climbing gear. Her cheeks showed signs of the heat and the intensity of the climb.

"We can try walking slower, but time is not on our side." He started uphill and noted out of his peripheral vision she trudged forward at a slower pace.

"I'm trying to remember exactly what happened back at the cabin." She let out a moan when she stepped over a protruding tree root. "I fell and hit my head so it's a little sketchy."

He paused and checked the fire. "Show me where it hurts." Her dark brown, sad eyes caught him off guard. His heart went out to her being in this situation.

"Ouch. That's it." She ducked her head away from his touch.

"Paramedics will check you out once we're rescued." He stepped back and walked away. "I need you to stay strong. Gotta step it up or we will literally be toast." He tensed over the urgency to find a safe zone. Her constant need to stop slowed them down and put them in more danger.

He hadn't intended on coming across as insensitive. And it wasn't like him to get antsy. But between the adrenaline rushing through his bones and too many things on his mind, he was getting impatient. He must stay focused on the direction of the wind and the attitude of the fire. He blamed the increased stress partly on his lack of sleep from studying the last few nights and the impending final grade that would make him eligible for the GS-5 ground-level forestry position. Not to mention the adrenaline crash after rescuing a busload of kids from a burning vehicle after it ran off the road late yesterday and caught the forest on fire. His fire team put out the blaze and was relieved the children escaped harm. His ex-fiancée wouldn't have liked that situation, either. None of that mattered in the heat of the moment, and he had to focus on their safety.

The terrain grew rocky and harder to climb, but that didn't slow the chasing fire. He considered digging a fire line, but there was no time. A firefighter digging alone to fight off the roaring blaze was pretty much useless. He needed his handcrew. Instructions from his training came to mind.

Stay alert, remain calm, think clearly and act decisively.

Kendall reached for her hand, and she willingly slid her slender hand into his. He took a deep breath and blew it out slowly.

Give her a break. Like she said, she's out of her element.

Hot smoke and ash tossed in the wind and swirled in their faces. Haley coughed until her face turned red. She'd breathed too much smoke already, but there was nothing he could do about it. He pulled out a face mask and handed it to her. "Should have given this to you earlier. Might help block some of the smoke and keep you from inhaling too much."

The mask obscured all but her big brown eyes, staring up at him with concern. Her fear punched him in the gut. He turned away. He had a job to do.

"That's better." The brief twinkle in her eye showed she'd smiled, but quickly faded. "Thanks."

A suspicious roar like a speeding train alerted Kendall to the approaching danger. Every muscle in his body tensed. The wind grew stronger, confirming his assessment. He spun and glanced back. A fire tornado. Haley squeezed his hand, and he tightened his grip on hers. His pulse shot more adrenaline through his body.

"What's that?" She pointed behind them.

"Trouble. Big trouble." He tugged her behind him and started running, almost dragging her. "A fire whirl. It's like a small tornado filled with fire. Come on. We're on its direct path."

The whites of her eyes grew larger. They bolted for cover and hunkered down behind another large boulder with tall grass and scattered pine needles around its base. Not a good choice, but it would have to do for now.

God, if You're there, protect us.

He pulled her close and wrapped his arms tight around her. Could he protect her from the flying, burning debris? She scrunched down and covered her face with her hands. He buried his face in her hair as it tossed with the wind and slapped against his cheeks. They'd die if they didn't get to the lowest place possible. He searched the area. The heat's intensity was too much, and he had no intention of dying today. Where could they go? The fire was about to consume them.

Chapter Two

Haley sank into Kendall's embrace as he tried to protect her. The security of his closeness gave her a small sense of safety, but the unbelievable strength of the wind threatened to blow her away. She peeked through her fingers at the swirling debris. Leaves, pine needles, limbs and even small trees flew past them. She'd never heard such a loud and frightening roar. A sound she'd never forget.

"Hang on." His urgent tone unnerved her.

"I am." Her throat burned. "Will it go away?"

"They can last ten minutes to almost an hour, and they cause as much damage as a regular tornado, sometimes worse."

"Don't tell me that. I can't survive an hour of this intense heat and blistering wind." She glanced back at him. "Looks like the fire is chasing us."

"We've got to find another shelter." His hand found hers and they eased upright, slightly bent at the waist.

A buck and three does darted by them. She expected the animals to be airborne. Her eyes met with Kendall's serious stare. He nodded toward the passing wildlife.

"Follow them." He took off running with her in tow.

The wind fought against their every step. Her feet faltered over the rough ground, and she almost lost her house shoes. Too bad she wasn't given time to put on her jogging shoes. Not that she jogged much. Her lack of exercise and stinging muscles threatened her ability to keep running. If she lived through this wildfire, she'd renew her membership at the gym.

The wind intensified. They fought the invisible strength that almost knocked her off her feet. Her face mask ripped from around her ears and flew away. She'd never been in a tornado, but if this fire whirl was anything like real tornadoes, she never wanted to experience another one.

"Don't let go of me," she yelled over the horrific howl and squeezed his arm with her other hand.

"I won't, just hang on. There's a river up ahead."

She glanced behind her and fought against the panic rising in every fiber of her being. It was as though that thing had zeroed in on their location, determined to consume them. Wetness streamed from her eyes from the high winds and the swirling smoke.

"We're not going to make it." Her legs grew weak. Defeat crawled over her. How would her parents handle their only daughter being consumed by such a monster?

"Yes. We are." Kendall stopped at the edge of the river. "We have to jump."

"Are you serious? I don't like this." Her heart pulsated in her ears. "Lord, help us." Her dad taught her how to swim in a swimming pool, but this rapidly flowing river looked dangerous. Burn or drown. She had no other options.

Debris flew past them. The heat of burning tree limbs sailed by and dropped into the river. "How safe is it?" Something in the distance caught her eye. She jerked her head in time to spot four men as they dived into the water. Blake? Kendall's grip squeezed tighter and crunched her fingers together.

"Not safe at all, but we have no choice," he yelled. "Jump."

"You won't let go of me, will you? I'm scared." Her leg muscles tightened.

"I won't let go. Trust me. Now jump."

She squeezed his hand until it hurt, took in a deep breath and they jumped into the river. Her body stiffened at the sudden impact of the mountain's frigid water. A muffled scream emerged from under her breath. The powerful undertow tugged at her grip on Kendall's hand. Her fingers slipped down into his palm. His other hand tried to reposition her hand in his, but the water interfered. She slipped from his hold. Her chest ached from holding her breath too long.

Save me, Lord. I'm drowning.

Her body tossed in every direction. Was she upside down or right side up? She kicked her legs, fighting to get her footing as the river whisked her downstream. Her head popped up for a quick gasp of air before she was sucked down again. Her leg slammed against a rock. Fear and adrenaline overrode the pain. A visual of her parents flashed before her eyes. Her dad's surgery. Would she make it home? Her mom needed her. She had to fight. They'd be devastated if she never returned. This wasn't the way she wanted to die.

A firm grip latched onto her arm and heaved her through the water. Hope of survival surged through her body. Who came to her rescue? Kendall? Blake? It didn't matter, she just needed to get above water so she could breathe. She'd held her breath as long as she could. Bubbles seeped from her lips as she swallowed water.

The hand drew her closer. In a moment's time, a strong, muscular arm wrapped around her waist and held her close. The undertow slackened, and her head emerged from the river into calm waters. She coughed, spat and gasped for air. Her foot touched the rocks beneath her. She balanced herself and stood. Her legs wobbled in sequence with her shivering body.

"Haley." Kendall's voice seeped into her waterlogged ears. He scooped her into his arms and carried her to the shore.

Her emotions surged. At this moment, she loved the sound of his voice so much she could kiss him. She took in a deep breath, mixed with the smoke that still drifted through the air.

"Haley, are you okay? That was one strong undertow. Thank goodness I caught up with you." He set her on the ground and squatted beside her. His hand supported her back.

"Thought I was going to drown. I prayed for help, and you appeared." She held on to his arm with one hand and wiped hair and water mixed with tears from her face with the other. His strength and closeness relieved her distress. "That undertow was like a vacuum. It sucked me away from you. I couldn't hold on. My leg hit a rock, but I think it's okay. Where is the fire whirl now?"

"It fizzled out when it hit the water. I promised I wouldn't let go, and I didn't, but the intensity of the current pulled you away. You were gone as I tried to catch a grip. I ran down the riverbank, searching for you. Your foot shot out of the water, then disappeared again. That's when I tossed my pack on the ground and jumped in after you." He patted her back before he removed his hand. "The current almost got the best of me, too. I always keep my promises, but this time I failed you, and I feel bad about that. As much as we need a break, we can't take the chance. This fire is unpredictable. Are you up to keep moving?"

"It wasn't your fault. I've never felt the strength of water ripping me downstream like that. My body is rebelling and my leg aches, but I know we can't stay here." Her eyes cut up to his. Did he have the same caring ways when he wasn't working as he showed on duty? He broke eye contact. Just as well.

Her frayed emotions were messing with her, and vulnerability wasn't a good thing.

"We've got to find a way out of here. You pray for our safety and wisdom. If God is anything like my dad, he isn't happy with me, so he probably wouldn't listen." Kendall glanced around and picked up his fire line pack. "The river swept you downstream, right back into the burning forest. Come on." He pulled her to her feet. "We'll have to go this way."

Her bare feet found the rocky ground. "Oh no, I lost my house shoes. Lost the mask, too." Intense heat blew across the river into her face. "How am I supposed to run on this rough ground?" Panic hung in her throat.

A grimace appeared on Kendall's face. He dropped his pack again and dug in, pushing the orange jumpsuits aside. A pair of sport sandals appeared. "Maybe these will help. Probably too big, but they'll beat walking the terrain barefooted." His eyebrows lifted. "At least it's something."

Her jaw dropped. "Flip-flops?"

"Nope. Adjustable sport sandals for men."

"Why do you have these when boots are better?" She dropped them on the ground and slid her feet into them. They were too big. She tightened the Velcro strap across the top of her foot as tight as it would go. "Not too bad. Thanks. They are a little long, but I'm not complaining."

"Yeah, it's nice to take my boots off and have something cooler to walk around in after work. I like them readily accessible. Forestry firefighters have a little red bag they carry with all our personal toiletries inside, and we have clean clothing back at our tents where they set up our command center. Never know how many days I'll be at one assignment, so it's best to be prepared." He tossed the pack over his shoulder and slid his arms through the loops. "Let's go before we're trapped by this fire."

He'd rescued her again. First from the cabin fire, then from the fire whirl and now from drowning in the river. Not to mention, he saved her feet with his flip-flops, uh, sandals. She couldn't help but admire Kendall's bravery and tenacity. Didn't mean she fully trusted him outside of his firefighter job, but he'd earned her confidence to get her out of this burning forest. She reeled at his preparedness. Who'd have thought he'd have sandals in a fire backpack?

Thank You, Lord.

She followed behind Kendall and forced herself to step higher through the tall weeds. Twigs and small stones bit at her bare heels. Her eyes shifted in search of Blake and his friends. Had they spotted Kendall and her before they jumped into the water? Would they track them down?

"Hey, did you see the escapees back at the river? They jumped in upstream from us."

Kendall spun. His eyes widened and fixed on hers. "That means they're coming up behind us."

Tension squeezed Kendall's shoulders. His thoughts shot back to the news bulletin he'd heard on his truck radio this morning. Armed and dangerous. He regretted the haphazard, joking thoughts of capturing these guys single-handedly. No way did he want to encounter these guys. Forget the promotion or his dad's rejection. Forget being the town's hero. He had to get Haley out of harm's way and try to stay out of sight of these men.

"Can we hide and let them pass us?" Concern and apprehension filled her expression.

"If we didn't have an inferno racing toward us, it might be an option, but time isn't our friend right now. I'm sure they're running for their lives, too, and are following the only semi-safe path out of here—our direction. Which means they could pick up our trail."

She pushed him. "Go faster."

"Thought you were struggling to move." He stomped through the grass, pushed vines and low-hanging limbs aside and held them back for Haley. If it weren't such a serious situation, he might have laughed at her sudden burst of energy.

Small embers tossed with the wind and landed all around them, instantly igniting the dry ground. The sun would disappear behind the mountain soon and they'd be in more danger of walking through the forest on the rough, uneven terrain. They needed shelter to shield them through the night, if there were such a thing as a shelter from this angry fire.

"My legs are weak and achy, but I'm forcing them to keep going. I don't know how long I'll last."

He threw his hand up and pointed into the woods. "Shh. Bear."

She halted and grabbed his bicep, and a gasp hit his ears. "Did he see us?" Her whisper was so faint Kendall hardly heard her above the roar of the wildfire. "Will he come after us?"

The huge furry animal turned and looked at them. He slapped a paw in the air and growled, then stepped toward them.

"He definitely knows we're here." Kendall slowly reached behind him and slid his hand into the side pocket of his fire pack and pulled out bear repellant spray. "Don't make any sudden moves. Stand tall and try not to show your fear."

"You're kidding, right? I'm petrified." Her grip tightened, and her fingernails dug into his arm. "Do you have a gun?"

"No. I have bear repellant." He kept his eyes glued to the behavior of the bear.

"That means he has to get close enough for you to spray."

"Pretty much."

The bear stopped and growled again. He slapped his paw in the air again and stood on his back two legs. His head turned, and he sniffed the air at the same time a cloud of smoke blew past. He dropped to all fours and ran in the opposite direction.

Haley let out a loud huff. "Thank You, Lord. He didn't attack."

"This is one time I'm thankful for smoke. He smelled it and took off, searching for safety. Keep your eyes open in case he doubles back and follows us. He doesn't like the fire any more than we do."

"Doubles back?" Haley's breathless words revealed her fear. "I didn't need that warning."

Kendall waited until the bear was completely out of sight before continuing their journey. Haley released her grip but remained close behind him. The constant heat blowing around them was like being in a sauna with no place to cool down.

His radio filled with static and broke up the message.

"Simpson. Come in. What's your location?"

"Crossed the river." He looked at his compass. "Moving northwest. Location unknown."

"Get…heli…way." Static took over the radio.

"Could you understand what he said?" Haley leaned closer.

"I think he was trying to tell us that a helicopter is searching for us or on the way, but I'm not sure where the chopper will have enough room to land and evacuate us." He stepped over a moss-covered log and helped her over it. "We're in a dense area where it's hard to spot us from the air."

Now that she had calmed down some, her voice didn't have that panicked, gasping sound. Kendall had questions about what happened in her cabin, and he wanted to learn more about her. Maybe they could talk when they reached a semi-safe distance from the flames and he found a place for them to rest.

"Any idea how the fire started?" She dropped his hand and slapped at a bug crawling on her shirt-sleeve.

"Not yet. It had to be human error or lightning.

Since we haven't had a storm in the last week or so, my guess would be someone tossed a cigarette or dumped coals from a grill or something."

She drew in a quick breath.

He spun. "What? Did you start the fire?"

"No. Of course not, but it could have been my neighbors cooking on their grill or one of the escapees tossing their cigarette butts."

"Sounds about right." Kendall resumed their trek through the forest. More cracking noises burst out in the distance. So many trees fell victim to the destructive blaze and created more heat and smoke that swirled past with every gust of wind. They coughed and covered their noses and mouths with their hands.

Kendall stilled at the brief reprieve from dissipating smoke. The hum of the fire continued in the distance, and a smoldering smell filled the air. Maybe they were safe to stop for a bit. He searched around them and spotted large rocks mounting several feet high. Vines and tall grass intermingled between them. Dusk was on the horizon, and the area would be pitch-black in a matter of minutes, except for the taunting, flickering flames not too far away.

No way would he keep going in the dark unless the impending threat intensified. He studied the direction of the wind and the distance of the fire. His body rebelled. He could use a break, too. No need asking Haley if she was exhausted. The way her breath heaved and the way she threw one foot in front of the other spoke volumes.

He pointed. "This looks like a good place to stop.

It'll be dark soon. Sitting higher off the ground allows for a better view. Gives us a little leeway should any of the wildlife pass by. Might have to make another run for it if the flames flare up more."

"I just want to get out of here, but I've got to get off my throbbing feet. These sandals have rubbed a couple of blisters. Who am I to complain?"

He climbed up on a boulder and helped her up beside him before he took his pack off. She tossed her long hair with her fingers and fluffed at it. Not sure how much good it did with all the blowing debris. He admired her determination.

"Back at the cabin after they tied me up, gagged me and put me in my bedroom, they closed the door and left me in the dark. As morning filtered through the window, I remember hearing several rapid knocks at the front door. Then someone opened the door and yelled 'firefighter.' You, probably. Then there was a scuffle." She pursed her lips. "I couldn't get out of the bedroom to evacuate or to see what was going on."

"What happened after that?" He gazed at the way her lips moved when she talked. He scolded himself for admiring her and looked away.

"I backed up to the door and turned the knob with my hands still tied. Thick smoke filled the room and I could barely see. Somehow, I lost my balance. I think someone bumped into me and I fell. Next thing I remember is you carrying me out." She sniffed. "How can I ever thank you for saving me?"

Was she about to cry? He was better at fighting

fires than he was consoling a crying lady. His fire-fighting training and experience with the Forest Service paid off in the rescue, but he hadn't expected to find a lady that piqued his interest.

He cleared his throat and studied the distant fire. "No need to thank me. It's my job and my honor to get you to safety."

Kendall opened his pack and pulled out the water bottle. "Have another drink. I'm sure you need it." If they weren't stuck in the forest, he'd guzzle the water down and soothe his dry, scratchy throat. A swallow or two would have to do until the rescue team came.

She turned the container up and gulped about four swallows, then handed it back. He took a couple of drinks, closed it up and returned it to the pack.

"Mind if I ask you a personal question?" He wiped the excess water from his mouth.

"Not at all."

Darkness dropped over the forest like the sudden pull of a window shade.

"Why were you in the cabin, out here in the mountains, alone? The wilderness isn't a place for anyone to be alone." He was fully aware of her sitting beside him. Their shoulders touched and her warmth soaked through to his skin. "Even though the mountains are beautiful and peaceful, there are still dangers." A bug hit his face. He slapped it away.

"My best friend became ill and couldn't make the trip. I tried to reschedule, but it was too late, and I'd put a large deposit down. They informed me I'd lose it if I canceled." She inhaled and let it out slowly. "None of my other friends were available, so I winged it and came by myself. Bad idea. I know it now and won't ever do it again."

"Couldn't your husband or boyfriend have taken some time off? I would be worried about my girl-friend hiking, camping or mountain climbing alone. It's just not safe." He suddenly realized he'd been admiring her and didn't even know if she was married. He kicked himself for the thought. He'd never interfere with someone's marriage.

"Well, that would have been nice, but I'm not married, and I booted the guy I was dating out of my life. Seemed he had a two-timing problem. I found out he was married and had kids. Can you believe the audacity?"

Kendall let out a low whistle and a sigh of relief. He'd just been vindicated from his admiration of her. "Pretty brazen."

"Yeah, well, next time I meet a guy, he'll have to prove himself trustworthy before I agree to date. People don't seem to care these days. That's why it's important to pray and stay in tune with God. Not that I'm a good example. I fail in so many ways."

"That's where I have a problem. I know God is out there, but I see him like my real dad, who doesn't approve of anything I do." That's all he needed to say about that. He hadn't intended on getting into God stuff.

"He's not like that at all. God is loving and understanding, and…" Her words halted.

Several twigs snapped. Crickets chirped, and the

occasional hoot of an owl reminded him they weren't alone. Her hand gripped his arm. He put his hand on top of hers and turned his ear toward the noise. They hadn't been loud, but hadn't whispered, either. Had the escapees found them?

Chapter Three

Haley's insides quivered. Who or what was out there in the darkness, coming toward them? Could it sense her fear? Kendall's warm hand offered reassurance, but it didn't calm the apprehension mounting.

Her breath faltered. Kendall's thumb tenderly raked across her knuckles. He eased away from her side. She blinked and tried to focus in the dark to see what he was doing.

A flashlight popped on. A buck and a doe stood in the thicket below them. Their heads lifted, and they froze in place. Large green, round eyes reflected toward them. The deer turned and darted into the blackness of the forest. Kendall turned off the flashlight.

She released the breath she'd stifled and pressed a hand against her chest. "Deer. You do not know how my mind played tricks on me. I imagined wild animals or the convicts." She removed her hand from her chest and placed it on the cool stone surface.

"Had an idea it wasn't anything dangerous, but I needed to make sure." His voice was barely audible. "Noises travel farther than we think out here in the wild. I had wondered if the escapees caught up with us, too."

She yawned. The lurking odor of smoke drifted closer. His hand found hers again. Amazing how his touch calmed her. He lifted his hand and patted the top of hers. "Why don't you lean against me and try to get some rest? I'll stay awake and monitor the fire and our surroundings."

"Do you really think I could sleep right now?" She yawned again.

"Sounds like you could." A muffled chuckle reached her ears.

He placed his fingers on the side of her head and eased it down until her head rested on his shoulder. His thoughtfulness tugged at her heart. She'd never experienced such tenderness, except for the open arms of her mom. She looped her arm through his and closed her eyes.

The flutter of wings jerked her awake, accompanied by a gasp.

Kendall tightened his arm against hers. "It's only a bat. They love the dark."

"A bat? Will they attack?" The hair on the back of her neck prickled.

"Not usually. But you can thank them for devouring mosquitoes." His even tone put her nerves at ease.

She removed her arm from around his and rubbed her eyes. "What time is it?"

"Ten after three. Won't be long until sunrise."

His warm breath hit her face. She couldn't see him, yet she imagined how romantic it would be if he kissed her right there in the wilderness, running from wildfire, avoiding dangerous criminals and animals while trying to survive. It was a dreamy thought but not realistic, like the fight scenes in a movie. The actors would pause for a kiss, then continue fighting the bad guys.

A sudden gust of wind pummeled them and grew in strength. Thickening smoke filled their nostrils. The blaze exploded in the not-too-far distance and the fire spread like fresh fuel had dropped on top of it.

"We've been here too long." Kendall jumped off the rock and helped her down.

"Will it catch up with us?" A chill raced down her spine. She'd assumed they were out of danger and waiting for the helicopter to rescue them. But being out in the middle of nowhere, there was no way to know what would happen next. Her life was in God's and Kendall's hands.

"If the wind keeps this up, then yes, we are in trouble." His hand slipped into hers and he turned his flashlight on. "Let's go."

"Wait." She released his hand and retightened the strap of his sandal on her foot.

He put the beam of light on her foot. "Are they still working for you?"

"Better than being barefooted. Like I said, they've rubbed a couple of blisters, but I can't complain." She straightened. The muscle in her leg that smacked a rock in the river ached. Haley took in a slow breath to avoid inhaling a gulp of smoke. Her throat and sinuses burned. "I'm ready."

He took her hand. "After daylight, I'll look at those blisters on your feet. Watch your step. It's treacherous in the dark."

Brush and vines raked across the top of her foot, and an occasional stick found her toes. Unidentified foliage scraped across her arms. No telling how many cuts and bruises she had, and she didn't want to know how much poison ivy and poison oak she'd encountered. Her body itched all over. Hopefully nothing a hot shower wouldn't cure, she surmised. Last time she had poison ivy on her leg, she had to have a cortisone shot.

Had her parents heard about the blaze on the news?

Lord, please don't let them go into a panic. My dad's heart may not be strong enough to handle the news, knowing my life is in danger.

A loud swoosh caught her attention. "How long will it take the fire to reach us?" Her voice cracked. "I can see the flames mixed in with the heavy smoke."

"Fire travels fast in the right conditions. Now that it's fall, leaves, pine needles and a lot of the ground cover have turned brown and are prime for igniting easily. I've seen flames travel from six to fourteen to twenty miles per hour and can go in unpredictable directions." He kept his pace as he talked.

"You are not helping my anxiety. We can't run

that fast." She increased her pace. Her ankle shifted in the uneven ground. *Ouch.* She focused on being sure-footed and walked closer to him. "How much longer before sunrise?"

The blue light on his watch lit up. "About two more hours, but we should start seeing signs of sunrise over the top of the mountain in about an hour and a half."

"That's still too long." She glanced behind her again and bit her lip. Uncertainty of survival threatened her emotions. She choked back tears and thought it would help if she changed the subject. "Tell me about yourself. You haven't mentioned your family other than your dad. Do you have a girlfriend or a wife?"

"Duck. There's a low-lying limb here. Don't let it hit you in the face."

She grabbed the branch. "Thanks for the warning."

"My mom is one of those energetic types. She loves to cook, shop and run around with her friends. Dad and I were the best of friends before I announced I was going to become a Forest Service firefighter. After that, my relationship with him spiraled downhill and now it doesn't matter what I do, it's never enough." His sweaty hand loosened, then re-gripped hers. "He can't get past our near-death experience when our house caught on fire years ago. He considered it an insult and slap in the face for me to choose to fight forest fires and willingly put my life in danger."

He continued, "I almost married several months ago, but she decided she didn't like the constant dangers of my job, so she bailed. Said she wasn't going to live a life of fear. Guess it wasn't meant to be. Probably for the best, considering my job is dangerous. But I love the challenge of fighting fires, saving people and the wildlife, and the camaraderie of my team."

Her thighs and calves stung. "We're climbing again. I can feel it in my legs."

"Yep. As soon as the sun comes up, I'll get my map and see if I can figure out where we are. Need to evaluate the direction of the wind and decide what route to take so the helicopter can get to us."

His comment about the dangers of his job and his girlfriend dumping him because of it distracted her. Sad that the girl had expected him to give up the job he loves. Her foot caught on a protruding tree root. She tripped, jerking her hand from his, and plunged to the ground. "Ouch. That hurt. There are rocks down here."

"Yep. Rocks are everywhere. Are you hurt?" His flashlight beam shot to the ground where she lay. "Is that blood on your pants?"

Haley lifted the leg of her lounge pants. "It's just a scrape. I'll be fine." She shoved the fabric down, covering her leg again. The wound throbbed and stung, and warmth rolled down to her ankle, but she refused to whine. She pushed to her feet and brushed dirt and leaves from her clothes.

Kendall's radio screeched. "Firestorm developing. Get…" His radio went silent. He shook it. Silence. "The battery is dead. It only lasts about sixteen hours."

Haley cringed. "Is a firestorm as bad as it sounds?" *Please say no.*

"You don't want to know. We call it that because it develops its own wind and can create surface indrafts that are small tornado-like whirls. Heat from a forest fire is hot, as you well know, but the overall heat intensifies in a firestorm."

A light glow of the sunrise filtered through the smoke and allowed a visual of Kendall. He took his hard hat off and raked fingers through his hair before he put it back on. His furrowed brow and intense stare into the forest spoke louder than words.

"That, uh, doesn't sound good. Is there enough light to see your map now?" Was it possible they were closer to a clearing by now?

"I think so." He swung his fire pack around. The weird tool that hung in a loop banged against a tree. He dug inside and retrieved a small map. His finger swiped over the paper in circles until he stopped. "I think we are in this area. If I'm right, we need to continue uphill, which is not in our favor, but we have limited options."

He put the map back inside the pack and slid his arms through the shoulder harnesses, tossing the bulky pack onto his back again. How he kept from hitting himself with that tool she didn't know. Experience, she supposed.

He turned and looked into her eyes, cupped his hands on her cheeks and leaned in. Was he going to kiss her at a time like this? Earlier, thoughts of him kissing her with all the danger sounded romantic, but not now. She sucked in a breath and waited for his next move.

"Haley, you can trust me. I will get you out of here. Try to lighten up with that scared, tension-filled expression." He kissed her forehead. "You pray, and I'll guide us to safety."

She blew out a huff. "I can do that." A kiss on her lips wouldn't have been so bad after all. His closeness helped ease her fears. Maybe next time, if there were a next time.

He trekked uphill through the rough terrain, making his own path. She lifted her feet as high as possible over the thick foliage and followed close behind him. Overgrown ferns sprinkled throughout the forest, still unaffected by the fall season.

She halted. "Did you hear that?"

"What?" He spun and stilled.

"Thought I heard voices."

Kendall suspected the convicts were closing in on them. His radio battery died a little while ago and his cell phone's battery was in the red and one bar flickered on and off.

"Can you call for help?" Haley stood, wide-eyed, staring at him.

"I can try." He found his handcrew leader's number and pressed the button. His pulse increased with anticipation when it rang, but then there was a squelch and it went dead. He clenched his jaw. They were on their own.

Disappointment loomed on her face. His sentiments exactly. But they weren't defeated yet, and the men still weren't in sight. They'd had time to put a little more distance between them as long as the men hadn't hiked through the night.

He touched her shoulder. "Want me to look at those blisters now?"

"No. I'll let you know when they're getting bad."

"Okay. We're going to keep moving while I try to come up with a plan. They'll catch up with us if we keep standing here." He dropped his hand and started walking. "How did you hear voices above the roar of the fire?"

"I don't know." She shrugged her shoulders. "Guess I've gotten used to the sound, and the voices interrupted the roar. Who knows? I've always had a keen sense of hearing. Hope I'm wrong, though."

Hiding and letting the convicts pass might be an option, but all that lay before him was a thick forest of trees, wild ferns, vines and rolling, uneven terrain, not to mention the fiery threat trailing behind them. They'd already passed the area of rocks and boulders that might have sufficed for a hideout.

"Those guys can't be walking the same way we are because there's not a path through here for them to follow unless one of them has experience or a tracking device. We're going through uncharted ground." He pointed to his left. "Look, a white-tailed deer. We're headed in the same direction. Must be a good sign."

Boom!

The ground shook.

Kendall came to a sudden halt and looked behind him.

"What was that?" Haley clutched onto his shirt.

"An indicator that means we have to make a run for it." He grabbed her hand and ran through the forest faster than her legs wanted to move. She stumbled a few times but found her footing. "It's the blowup my team warned us about. A sudden rush of flames and fiery wind from the wildfire's explosion. If we don't find adequate cover, well, we're done."

"Oh no." Her breath came out in huffs as she ran behind him. "The roar is incredibly louder than before."

"Like I said, 'you pray.'" A sense of urgency rushed through him. Time was of the essence.

A small dip in the earth came into view. The pounding in his chest reverberated in his ears. A small refuge from the approaching blast of thermal wind. He jumped down into the three-foot dip and retrieved his fire shelter bag. He crawled inside and opened it for her to scoot in as close as possible next to him. He zipped it closed as far as he could reach in the confined space and had her reach back and finish closing it. He couldn't hold her any closer than they already were. The two of them barely squeezed inside. A shift in the wind offered a slight reprieve from a direct hit of the approaching fiery wall.

He lay on his side and put his arm around her. "Pull the neck of your top up over your mouth and breathe the air close to the ground so the radiant heat and smoke doesn't scorch your lungs."

"I'm scared." She tugged at her top, then folded her arms and leaned into his chest. "Lord, protect us, please."

He covered his mouth and pressed himself to the ground with her.

God, help us.

Hot air surrounded him. The all-too-familiar sound of a firestorm blew overhead. His entire body beaded with sweat and soaked his clothes as the radiant heat roared past. Haley let out a muted scream. Her cries ripped at his heart, but there was nothing more he could do. He prayed God heard their prayers. He squeezed her close and patted her back with his fingers. Not much comfort considering the seriousness of their situation.

Minutes seemed like hours before the roar subsided somewhat. Kendall had her pull the zipper down as far as she could, then he finished opening the bag. He pulled the protective bag back far enough for him to ease his head up. Was it safe to emerge from their cover? He pushed to his knees beside her. Heat lingered, but they'd survived the worst. Had God heard their prayers and turned the direction of the wind?

He stood with his collar pulled up over his mouth and nose, checking the condition of the forest and the extent of the fire. Smoldering grass and burning trees surrounded them. Thick smoke boiled in the air. The back of his sleeve and pants legs looked scorched. Pieces of Haley's clothing had a melted look, but for the most part, the fire shelter protected them from burns.

"You can come out now." He helped her up. "Keep your nose and mouth covered."

She rolled over and sat up. "We survived."

"Thanks to your prayers." He wiped rolling sweat from his face.

"Prayers and your expert, quick thinking."

Dried leaves and dirt mixed with perspiration and tears formed small spots of mud on her red face, accentuating the whites of those chestnut-colored eyes. Her brown, matted hair fell over her shoulders.

He helped her stand and pulled debris from her hair. Her gaze seemed to go right through him. He considered pulling her into his arms, holding and comforting her, but he'd be out of line showing affection while on duty. He hadn't counted on being attracted to her.

She leaned against him, put her arm around his waist and squeezed. He reciprocated the embrace and enjoyed every second of her closeness.

"Thank you for saving me for the third or fourth time." She backed away with tear-filled eyes and looked at the sky. "Lord, thank You for hearing our prayers and saving us."

"I think you got it right the second time. God heard your prayer." He uncovered his nose and smoke filled his nostrils. He coughed, then picked up his scorched pack and Pulaski tool. The handle had a few burned streaks, but survived as well. He held it with one hand and helped her out of the small gully with the other, thankful his folding combi tool was in his pack in case the handle broke on his Pulaski.

She bent over and coughed and gasped for breath. He retrieved his thermos.

"Here. Have a drink. It will help you stop coughing." He poured a few drops of water on a bandanna he'd stuffed in his bag. It would help block the smoke and keep her from coughing too much.

He studied the map and guessed about where they were now after making a run for it. Sweat rolled down his back. "If I'm reading correctly, we can go west from here. The biggest part of the fire appears to be moving northeast, but that can change with the wind."

"Does that mean we're heading out of the burn area?" She bent and brushed dirt from her pants like it helped. She glanced up at him with a questioning look.

He withheld a smile at her attempt at cleanliness. A hot shower with the water pounding his tense shoulder muscles would feel great right about now. Not to mention a T-bone cooked medium-well. The pop and sizzle of a burning tree brought him back to reality.

"Don't worry about your clothes. You look fine. I mean, look at me. It's the best we can do under the circumstances."

"I'll be glad when we're in the clear."

Kendall straightened his shoulders and rolled his neck until it popped. "That's my goal. To get us in the clear. You ready?"

"I guess." She retightened the straps on the sandals.

He stuffed the compass in his pants pocket and the map in the side slot of his pack. His Pulaski still hung in the large loop on his bag. The smoking ground had him keeping a check on her feet. She hadn't mentioned it, but the rubber at the heels of the sandals had melted off. A grim reminder of how closely the fire nibbled at their heels, literally.

Each calculated step moved them closer to a clearing. At least, that's what he thought he'd spotted in the distance. Haley pushed her sleeves up in the encapsulated heat zone. Perspiration continued rolling from her forehead. A focused, less fearful expression showed on her face. She'd handled their situation much better than he'd expected.

She'd mentioned God a few times, and he had, too. However, he hadn't decided if God had answered his prayer or hers. Examining the actions and attitude of his earthly dad had him relating the same traits with his heavenly father. He doubted his prayer counted. His dad's hurtful words echoed in his mind.

"You disappoint me. I built this business from the ground up and expected my son to take over one day," his dad had said. "Not for you to willingly put your life in danger, fighting fires that almost killed our whole family. Where are your family values?"

"But, Dad," Kendall reasoned. "My dream is to

be a Forest Service firefighter, not a welder. I want to help rescue people like the firefighters did to save us and I want to help protect the wildlife and save the forest from fires."

"I thought I knew you, but apparently I don't." His dad stormed away.

"You're quiet. Care to share what you're thinking?" A slight popping sounded with each step as rubber slapped against Haley's heels. The melted backs of his sandals made them fit her feet better.

"It was amazing how the wind shifted like it did in the blowout. In all sincerity, we wouldn't have survived back there." Kendall searched the terrain in the distance and monitored their every step. His handcrew, the jumpers and the rest of the group were searching for them. That, he was certain about. Had the escapees survived the blowout? He halted and faced Haley. "Did you hear that noise?"

She giggled and pressed her hand to her belly. "Sorry, that was my stomach. It seems to have an automatic buzzer that goes off when it knows I've missed a meal." Her shoulders shook when she laughed. "But I'm okay. We can do this."

"Oh, my bad." He reached back into a large side pocket and retrieved two granola bars, handing her one and keeping one for himself. "What kind of protector would I be if I let you starve to death?"

"I would chomp on a stick if I got that hungry." She bit into the bar. "Not bad. Thank you. Speaking of eating a twig, the convict named Mac had one in his mouth when they broke into my cabin. Maybe a stick isn't a good choice. I don't want to mimic him. Do you think they survived?"

Kendall held his finger to his lips. "I think I see something behind us."

Haley took a hold of his shirt and froze.

Chapter Four

A shiver rushed over Haley's body. She wanted the convicts to survive, but she didn't want to run into them again, even if one of them was her cousin. She'd prayed for Blake multiple times, but her encounter with him yesterday proved his rebellion and hardened heart. Not that she'd given up, not at all. She needed to pray harder for all of them. The men's lack of value for human life unnerved her. How could people be so cruel and calloused?

"Is it them?" She kept her grip on Kendall's shirt and stepped closer to him.

"I can't be certain. Although my gut says yes." His gentle touch on her arm pulled her hand away. "Can't waste any time. Let's keep moving."

She refused to complain about his fast pace, although it was difficult to keep up with him while wearing his sandals that continued rubbing the already irritated blisters. The stride of his long legs equaled two of her steps. She ran to keep up with him. He had an admirable work ethic, but his compassion and caring attitude warmed her and helped calm her unsettled nerves. He protected her even during a deadly situation.

From what she'd already witnessed about Kendall, he differed from other men she'd known. She wondered what it would be like to get to know him in a non-crisis situation.

Her leg muscles burned with the constant movement and gradual incline. She'd do anything to avoid flaming, falling trees. Many of them stood tall like a toothpick, stripped of all their leaves while fire swallowed up the ground vegetation around them. Her feet turned black with soot from all the ashes. The scrapes on her feet throbbed. No telling what her face looked like at this point.

"Haley, how are you holding up?" Concern filled Kendall's voice. "I think we're approaching an area that hasn't burned."

"We're alive and that's all that matters. How about you?" Telling him she was tired, her legs didn't want to move anymore, her throat was sore from inhaling smoke, her feet ached from pokes and scrapes from twigs and rocks and she was hungry wouldn't help move them forward or get them rescued. If he was half as tired as she was, he was beyond exhausted and starved.

"I'm trained to endure hardships in the forest, but this is the first time I've had to run from a large fire whirl, dive into the rapids of a river to keep from burning alive, bury myself in my fire shelter and pray I survive, all while protecting a beautiful dam-sel in distress. Does that answer your question?" He looked back at her, exposing his smile and dirty face, then covered his mouth and nose again.

"Completely. I'd argue the damsel-in-distress part, but this time I think you've got me pegged. I wouldn't be where I am if you hadn't found me in the cabin." Her heart warmed at his attempted humor.

They emerged into a fresh, unburned part of the forest. Green, red, yellow and orange leaves deco-rated the forest like a beautiful painting. Who could deny God's creative canopy? Haley gazed at the col-orful palette set before her. Such beautiful scenery amid a destructive force.

She drew in a despairing breath. The flames trailing behind them jumped from tree to tree while burning grass and leaves tossed with the breeze, ig-niting more fires. She removed the bandanna from her face for a moment of fresh air, then put it back on.

"Now that we can rest a second, I need to check my backpack again for extra radio batteries. I couldn't find them in the dark and we've been on the run since." Kendall dropped his pack and dug deep into the bag. He pulled out a pair of socks from the bottom of the bag. "Oh, here, put these on. They will help protect your feet. Here's a small first aid kit. Let's put Band-Aids on those popped blisters."

"Wow. Too bad I didn't have these socks ear-lier. Well, probably a good thing, since the blowout singed everything. The socks would have melted on my feet." She sat on the ground in the tall weeds and let Kendall doctor her feet, then she slid the socks on. "These make the sandals fit snug. Maybe I can move faster."

"Good. I should've thought about them before now." He kept digging in his bag. "This is ridiculous. I keep my bag organized so everything is easily accessible." He rose up and looked at her. "One more pocket. If the batteries aren't in there, then I don't have any. Keep a watch behind us."

Haley turned and stared into the depths of the forest where they'd just escaped. The burned trees with black limbs stretched to the sky and looked so desolate. Sad what the fire had done to the beauty of the mountains. "No sign of the convicts so far. Maybe they went another direction."

"Yes. I found them." Kendall retrieved his radio and inserted the new batteries. His radio came to life. "Simpson here, are you guys still out there?"

"Hey, man, where are you? We thought you and the girl were goners. Give us your location. We'll send a chopper."

Haley wanted to dance and squeal. They'd contacted Kendall's team and help would arrive soon. She blew out a slow breath and dropped her shoulders. What an intense experience, and her firefighter hero would get all the credit. He deserved an award or something for his quick thinking and bravery.

The gleam in Kendall's eyes said it all. He was relieved, too. "Don't know the exact location, but follow the west side of the blowout. We're somewhere in that area."

"On it. How'd you get that far up the mountain? Any sign of the escapees?"

"Running, that's how. Spotted them twice, but not since the blowout. Not sure of their status."

Haley could hardly contain herself. Help was on the way. Her parents didn't have to plan a funeral, and she'd make it to her dad's heart surgery. *Thank You, Lord. I trusted You and You showed up.*

The wind blew her hair one direction when they'd come out of the burn zone, but suddenly her hair whipped the other direction. Her breath caught. She'd learned enough from hanging out with Kendall in this short time to pay attention to the direction of the wind.

She widened her eyes and stared at him. "Kendall."

"The wind changed directions and I feel an updraft. Gotta run. Get here ASAP." He jumped to his feet with the radio in hand. "Not good. The fire will shift now and we're still in its path. Let's go."

Her mouth went dry. She'd celebrated too soon. With her back to the wind, the heat of the fire bore down on her. His socks were softer on her feet, but they did nothing for her tired leg muscles. Just when she thought she couldn't take another step, he reached back and took her hand, pulled her up to his side and forced her to run with him. Even now, he still cared about her safety when he could protect himself.

Something off to the side caught her attention. Dread consumed her. "No. Please. It can't be." Four men ran from behind some boulders and shot at them, shouting for them to stop. Haley screamed and covered her head with her hands. "Stop it." Bullets hit the ground by their feet and drew them to a sudden halt.

Kendall lifted the radio and held the bottom half in his hand. "Escapees found…" A gunshot shattered the top of his radio. Pieces of plastic flew in different directions, making minor cuts on his face and a larger cut on his hand. Her stomach plummeted. The men had obliterated their only resource for rescue.

The shooting stopped, and the men rushed toward them. She took off her bandanna and checked the cut on his face. Blood rolled down his cheek from a couple of slight cuts. A small gash near his thumb looked a little deeper, but they weren't anywhere near a medical facility. She glared back at the three escapees and the other guy with them. If looks could kill, well, she wouldn't do that, but she'd send them back to prison. She tightened her lips, propped her hands on her hips and stared at them.

"What do you think you are doing?" she yelled above the roar of the flames coming their direction. "He's our only way out of here and you could've killed him."

The four men approached, three with their weapons pointed at them. One man wore a prison guard uniform. Blake jerked the Pulaski from the loop on Kendall's pack. "Wouldn't want you getting any ideas."

"Why don't all of you just go on ahead and leave us alone?" Haley fumed.

"Feisty, isn't she?" Mac grinned.

"Aw, cuz, you wouldn't want your favorite relative to get hurt, would you?" Blake gripped her arm. She jerked it away.

"I don't wish harm on anyone, but you and your friends could mind your own business and go hide wherever you're going. You'll have to hide for the rest of your lives." She pressed her lips together before she blurted more out at her cousin and his so-called friends.

Kendall's eyebrows lowered with a questioning look on his face. "Your cousin? That's right. You mentioned one convict was a relative, but you never answered my question."

Suddenly, like a punch to her own morals and virtues, shock and horror gripped her. She'd intended to clear the air with Kendall about her innocence in the escapees' arrival and how Blake said he'd found her. But they'd been on the run, and she hadn't given it another thought. Trust and honesty were the very things she desired in a man and Kendall showed just that, at least so far. She hadn't lied. She just hadn't found the opportunity to inform him of her cousin's ruthlessness.

"Haley, did you help them escape?" The disappointment in Kendall's eyes cut deep.

"Yeah, Haley, did you help us? He wants to know," Blake mocked. The others with him laughed.

"Stop it, Blake. You know, good and well, I've

had nothing to do with you since you chose a life of crime. I never even visited you in prison, so get over yourself." Heat rushed to her face, and it wasn't the fire.

Mac grabbed both of her arms from behind. "You gonna let her talk to you like that, Blake? Thought you could handle her."

"Let her go. She's all talk. She won't do nothing." Blake pushed Mac's arms away and put his arm around her shoulders and smirked. "She's one of those churchgoing girls, but look at her now. She's not acting like a saint."

She shoved him away and glanced at the approaching flames. "I'm not perfect, but I strive to do what's right. You should've paid attention when your mom made you go to church. Now it looks like fire and brimstone is going to get us all." Haley turned to Kendall. "I should've told you what happened, but when you said you'd found the orange jumpsuits in my car, I could tell you suspected I was involved. I didn't think you'd believe I had nothing to do with his escape."

She waited for Kendall's response, but before he opened his mouth, the wind swirled with more force and the fire crept in their direction like a lion focused on its prey. How had she grown so attached to this handsome firefighter? Her heart grieved. He thought she'd deceived him, just like she'd grieved over being deceived by the lies of her ex-boyfriend.

She hadn't meant to cause friction between Kendall and her.

* * *

Kendall wiped the blood from his cheek. The two cuts on his face stung, but the one on his hand smarted the worst. Nothing he couldn't handle. She'd mentioned one of the convicts was her cousin but hadn't elaborated. True, he'd been suspicious that she had helped them get away and then allowed them to tie her up and gag her so it would appear she was a victim.

Although it didn't make sense for them to tie her up and leave her. The forest and her cabin were on fire. They'd left her unconscious on the floor. What kind of cousin would leave a relative behind like that? Maybe her explanation about the situation wasn't so wrong after all.

He wanted her to be innocent of the whole affair now that he'd grown to like her. But how could he trust someone who withheld vital information?

Her reaction to the one called Blake convinced him she told the truth. However, it still bothered him she hadn't even tried to explain what happened. He'd still have to mull it all over and decide whether to believe her.

He stiffened at the flare-up of flames about to consume them.

"Unless you guys have a death wish, we need to put some distance between us and this fire. The grass burns faster than you think, and that fire will be on top of us in a matter of minutes." He eyed them, turned and started walking.

"Where do you think you're going?" Mac rushed up beside Kendall.

"To safety." Kendall tightened his jaw. "Haley, come on. Let these guys make their own decisions."

Haley rushed to Kendall's side. He still wasn't sure how he felt about the whole thing with her, but he certainly didn't want any harm to come to her. These men had caused enough havoc.

The four of them followed, grumbling along the way.

"You'd better not try anything." Connor finally spoke up. "Should have done away with her while we had the chance. We have this firefighter now. If he makes a wrong move, she'll have to pay."

Kendall shot a disgusted look back at the men who stomped behind him with their weapons in a ready position. Although his nerves were on edge with these trigger-happy escapees, he wasn't about to reveal his fears. One move misjudged by them could cripple Haley and him or kill them both. "Nobody's getting hurt on my watch. The only thing I'm trying to do is to save us all from burning alive. Now pick up the pace if you want to live." With no backtalk, he'd been successful in his approach to their threats.

Who would have thought a prison guard would get involved? What was in it for him? Money? There was no hiding his identity unless he stole the shirt. His uniform had his name embroidered above the pocket. Officer J.R. Graham. And he carried a small blue backpack on his back. His lack of loyalty to his government position angered Kendall. No respect.

The guy stepped so close to Kendall he was certain J.R.'s bad breath could cause a tree to wither and fall on its own.

Blake chuckled. "Should've seen the shock on her face when we broke into her cabin. After she realized she had three unexpected guests, a different type of fire burned in her glare." He twirled the Pulaski around and let it hit the ground.

His friends chimed in and joked about her being leery of them. "We could've yelled, 'Boo,' and she would have passed out," Mac said. "She feared us. Good to know we can intimidate people like that. They'll do what we say, or they won't see tomorrow."

Kendall shot a glance at Haley. The solemn look on her face hadn't changed as she rolled her eyes at the harassment. Was he being too hard on her, too?

He refocused on the forest before them and searched for signs of his crew or for evidence of rangers, jumpers or sawyers. Not a helicopter in sight. No humming sounds of an airplane. Now that the guys destroyed his radio and his phone battery had died, he was at the mercy of his team's judgment and perceived direction to find them.

"Better get a move on, fire boy, we're about to be crispy critters if you don't find us a place to hide." Mac removed the twig, spat on the ground and put it back in this mouth. "I didn't escape prison to die out here."

"Doing the best I can." Kendall's words stuck to the roof of his dry mouth. The last thing he needed was these guys belittling his forestry and firefighting knowledge while counting on him to save them. How twisted could the whole scenario get?

In the distance, a small river came into view. Nothing like the raging one Haley and he had encountered earlier. He couldn't lose her like that again. The way the fire moved toward them the river might be a good option, or their only option, for distancing themselves from the blaze.

A sudden hissing sound popped as flames ignited in the tall trees and embers dropped to the ground. The undergrowth burst into flames and consumed the ground cover. Gusts of wind tossed the embers in different directions and thick, black smoke swirled into the sky. Trees sizzled. One cracked and fell against another. An added danger that goes with wildfires.

Kendall fought against frustration. Now he had to deal with four rebellious adults who thought only of themselves. He couldn't let anyone die, but he'd make sure Haley stayed safe. These men were big enough to take care of themselves.

"Come on." He walked faster. "There's a river ahead. We need to get to the other side before that tree falls. This entire area will go up in flames in a matter of minutes."

Haley kept the pace. He reached for her with his good hand, and she took it. The ground was rough and had a lot of uneven dips, making it a potential risk for a twisted ankle or, worse, breaking a bone. Haley stumbled, but quickly straightened and kept walking. The guys behind him went into a slow trot.

"Hey, fire boy," J.R., the guard, yelled above the increasing roar of the fire. "Just remember, if we go down, you and the girl are going down with us. I suggest you don't try any of your fire tricks on us."

What? Was he really questioning Kendall's expertise? Sure, the fire was a definite threat, and he was doing his best to keep Haley and himself alive. Kendall's stomach churned. J.R. didn't deserve a response. He'd try saving their lives, but he couldn't be responsible if they didn't succumb to his professional firefighting training.

A small rolling hill took them down to the river, which would pass as a large stream. He stepped into the cold water. Slick rocks lined the bottom. The undertow tugged at his legs, but nothing like before.

Haley sucked in a breath. "Whoa, who knew this water could be so icy? Big change from walking through a forest sauna."

Splashes sounded behind Kendall. He inspected everyone's position in the water.

"This ain't the bath I wanted." Connor waded deeper. "I prefer showers. Beats the inferno, though."

"Are there fish in here?" Blake chimed in and put his face close to the water, using the Pulaski to steady him.

Mac shoved Blake's head under water. Blake popped up and pushed Mac. Mac shoved Blake. Blake lifted Kendall's tool into the air like he'd was going to slam Mac.

Connor and J.R. laughed.

"Get him," J.R. yelled.

Blake lowered the tool and dived for Mac. They both went underwater, punching each other while the other two placed bets on who would win.

Haley placed her hand on Kendall's arm. They exchanged glances and shook their heads. "Such a piece of work," Kendall said. "Like we don't have enough to worry about."

"What are we going to do?" Haley whispered.

"Let them fight while we stay alive." Kendall waded deeper into the water, holding Haley's hand. He hadn't figured the river would be deep. He'd reached the middle, and the water struck him at his chest. Haley's eyes widened a bit. The water sloshed at her chin. Her other hand gripped his shoulder as she pulled herself up higher, out of the water. "Don't worry. I've got you."

Fire rolled toward them like a ball and picked up speed. Experience confirmed these flare-ups could happen randomly.

He looked at Haley. "When I say 'now,' take a deep breath and go underwater."

Her expression calmed, like she trusted what he said. He admired her respect for his forestry firefighting knowledge.

He yelled at the men, "I suggest you pay attention to your real enemy." He pointed to the approaching fire. "Dunk underwater and count to thirty if you want to live."

Burning leaves and small limbs blew their direction. Several hit the water closer than was comfortable. He watched the fire approach and counted down, "Three, two, one." He squeezed Haley's hand. "Now," he said.

Her mouth opened, then closed. She went under the same time he did.

Kendall opened his eyes under the clear water. Flames shot across the river, then settled back to the bank. More debris fell over them. Amazing how the heat filtered underwater. He counted the seconds down in his head. Twenty-eight, twenty-nine, thirty. He tugged on Haley's hand and emerged into the swirling smoke.

Haley gasped and sucked in smoke, then went into a coughing fit. She pushed a couple of smoldering limbs away. The escapees were all coughing. He should have warned them about the smoke. He tugged at the bandanna that hung around her neck.

"Pull this back up over your mouth and nose so you don't inhale any more smoke. The heat can burn your lungs. It's wet, but it will help protect you." He zeroed in on her gaze and studied her.

"Hey, get away from my cousin," Blake yelled through his coughs. He leaned into the water, brought up Kendall's tool and shook it in the air.

Kendall curled his nose at him. "You left her to die. Don't try to make me think you care what happens to her now." The cut on his hand stung for a minute after being in the water, but quickly calmed down.

Blake rushed through the water toward Kendall. Mac stopped him. "Give it a rest. Let them enjoy whatever time they have left."

Blake slapped at the water and stomped out onto the other side of the river. His friends followed suit, wringing their wet clothes and grumbling.

Kendall moved through the river and eased onto the bank. Haley followed and squeezed water from her top and the bandanna, then covered her mouth and nose again.

He stomped the mud from his boots. His clothes would dry fast enough in the heat. He hadn't wanted to run into the escapees, and yet he had. He no longer wanted to capture them single-handedly, but the possibility was to be determined. They didn't scare him much, and he didn't want them hurting Haley. She didn't appear to be afraid to speak her mind around them, either. Would her cousin really let her die? Absurd. Where were the family values? Funny he should question their values when his dad had asked the same question and now they weren't speaking.

J.R. marched up to Kendall like a disgruntled child and put his pistol under Kendall's chin. "You enjoyed making us get into that icy river. You pull another stunt like that, and I'll make you pay." He stormed away.

"You're welcome." Kendall bristled. "I just saved your life."

"They're not going to listen to reason," Haley said. "We just have to pray for them."

Kendall lowered his brows and looked at her. "Pray for them? Really? We need to be praying for a rescue team to save us all."

"You know what I mean. They need an encounter with the Lord to soften those hardened, selfish shells they've encapsulated themselves in." She held wisdom in her soft tone.

"I suppose you're right." Spot fires surrounded them on the opposite side of the river. He'd have to keep his eyes open. Fire was so unpredictable. Fingers of fire extended in long, narrow extensions from the main body. He'd seen it before, and the danger was real.

Chapter Five

Haley had never encountered fire at such magnitude as this forest wildfire. In fact, the only actual fires she'd experienced were sitting around a cozy fireplace in the comfort of her apartment. Her fireplace warmed her in the winter and the sun kept her toasty in the summer. The intensity of heat that radiated from a forest fire had a singeing effect on her skin. This stuff was nothing to play with or take lightly.

Would they outrun the fire or become trapped and end up tomorrow's latest fatality story?

Stop. I refuse to think negatively. God, You've got this, right?

Kendall had every reason to be rude, curt or even angry, yet he maintained control of his emotions when the men harassed him. He had a right to question her innocence. She should've made sure he understood that Blake and those escapees hid in her cabin against her wishes. He'd been nothing but cordial, protective and respectful of her and the others. She studied him. The crease in his brow told her he was under pressure or uncertain about their situation. Maybe both.

"When I get out of here, I'm headed to California. I'm going to be a beach bum and watch all the beautiful babes walk by." Connor blew a kiss to the sky.

Haley rolled her eyes again. Such dead-end plans for a grown man.

J.R. brushed at his pants leg, then squeezed water from his small backpack and soaked wallet. "I'm headed to Mexico. They'll be looking for me after helping with the escape and I'm not going to prison where I've been hard on a lot of those prisoners."

"Guess you should treat people the way you want to be treated." Haley glanced over at Kendall. He'd gathered his pack and tossed it over his shoulder, ready to continue the journey. "That's what the Bible says. Do to others as you'd have them do to you."

"I don't need you preaching to me." J.R. bolted upright. His face fumed red.

"Time to move. We're not out of danger yet." Kendall spoke up at the right time. Otherwise, J.R. might have lashed out at her more.

Mac pushed to his feet after leaning against a tree. "You guys can do what you want. I crave the excitement of robbing banks and stores. I love having control of all those people and seeing the horror in their expressions. Once I get enough money, if there's such a thing, I'll settle down in Hawaii or the Bahamas."

Haley had first-hand knowledge of Mac's hostile intimidation, something she wouldn't succumb to again.

"You really think money will make you happy? Why would you want to hurt people like that?" Haley clamped her mouth shut. These guys were getting on her last nerve. So disrespectful. But God loved everyone the same, and she had her faults, too.

The men fell in behind Kendall and her as they made their way through the overgrown woods. While on the run, she could only pretend to understand how they imagined living their lives. Maybe she should pray they'll come to grips with reality.

"By the time we hike up and down these mountains and fight swirling waters, I just might get in shape after this involuntary workout." Haley pressed her palms to her knees, pushing herself upward with each painful, uphill step. She'd used more muscles in the last twenty-four hours than she remembered having. *Keep going. I can do this.*

Kendall grinned. "Lean into the climb, breathe slowly and deeply to decrease your heart rate. It helps your body take in the oxygen you need and helps fight symptoms of high altitude."

"It's educational hanging around you." Haley considered the forest ahead. "You said fire climbs uphill faster than down. When we reach the top of the mountain, will we be able to slow down since we will shift to going downhill?"

"It means you have limited time on this earth when we reach a safe place. I'm hungry and tired."

Connor's sudden outburst and arrogant tone challenged her self-control. He pressed his finger to her shoulder and pushed slightly. What was his problem?

She jumped to the side. "Don't touch me." She brushed at her shoulder like he'd put something there.

"Oh, copping an attitude, are you? Look who's holding the gun." Connor waved his weapon in the air.

"Leave her alone." Blake pushed Connor on the back. He'd held on to the Pulaski like it was a lifeline.

Connor pointed the gun at Blake. "Wanna make me?"

Blake didn't respond. "When I get out of here, I'm going to get a new ID and move to Oregon. I hear they've legalized marijuana there and it will put me miles away from everyone."

Haley glared at Blake. "You're big enough to make your own decisions, but I'd like to think you've learned some valuable lessons through all your trials at home and on the streets. You have a lot to offer if you'd think about someone other than yourself."

"Stay out of my business," Blake said.

"I'm praying for you." She pointed at the three other men. "These new friends of yours are only friends until they don't need you anymore. Then, they'd just as well shoot you, unless you see things their way."

"You gonna let her talk to you like that?" J.R. bowed up like the guard he should have been. "Back at the prison, I'd put her in the hole faster than she could spit."

"Stop your bickering. She's right and you know it." Kendall's lips tightened.

Guess she should follow suit and not be so mouthy. These guys were irritating.

Lord, help me control my tongue. Their selfishness makes me so angry.

The mountain view from the top was both beautiful and frightening. Rows of mountains rolled across the skyline in various shades of fall. Simply amazing. How could anyone not believe there was a God with the layout of His colorful canvas spread out like this? Yet, the view didn't show the location of a road or a town or civilization anywhere.

Haley looked behind her. They were in the middle of nowhere, with a rear view of the approaching blaze. She picked at her fingernail as she took in the wildfire's magnitude. It was like a huge U shape with them at the base of the U. The monstrous smoke cloud swirling high in the sky sent chills down her back like a slithering snake coiling around for the last squeeze. She shivered and her jaw dropped. Fire almost surrounded them. Her heart pounded. Could they possibly make it to the opening of the U before the sides closed in and blocked their escape?

"Will we continue hiking through the night, Kendall?" *Please say we can rest.* It didn't look feasible to stop and she wouldn't admit her exhaustion. They had enough whining going on.

It had been a long day, and the sun lowered close to the mountaintop in the distance. It would be dark soon. Kendall had told her last night that trying to hike the rough, mountainous terrain through the wilderness after dark was too dangerous, even though the fire steadily burned. Surely, they could find a safe place to stop for the night amid the turmoil of it all. She dreaded another night with these annoying men, except for Kendall. He didn't fall into that category. Dark smoke climbed to the heavens and exposed an orange sky each time the wind blew smoke aside.

"We're facing a double-edged sword. If we stop, the fire has no mercy and will continue to burn and move toward us. We are also at the mercy of the wind and atmospheric pressure, but trekking through the forest in the dark has its dangers, too.

"If I can find us a semi-safe place to rest a bit, I'll let you know. Unless we're forced to keep moving, I think everyone is ready for a break." He pointed to an area of boulders below. "We might be okay to stop over there. Let's check it out."

He proceeded downhill, but stopped abruptly and threw out his hand.

"What are we stopping for?" Mac stepped up beside Haley.

She pointed to a bear walking along the line of pine trees. "Be quiet."

"Oh." He lifted his pistol. Connor and J.R. stepped up and lifted their pistols.

"Stop." Kendall kept his hand in the air. "The bear is minding his own business. Just let him be. We don't shoot the wildlife unless it's necessary."

"Looks necessary to me," Connor said.

"No. Not unless he charges us." Kendall's voice lowered.

Kendall never ceased to amaze Haley. Not only was he protecting her and this group of men who continually threatened to kill him, he was protecting the wildlife as best as he could.

"I've got him in my crosshairs," Mac whispered.

Kendall reached out and pushed Mac's gun down. "I said don't."

Mac shoved Kendall backward. "Don't tell me what to do."

"Stop it." Haley tried to muffle her voice as not to upset the bear. "We don't need any more trouble. You guys are like a group of toddlers, bickering every chance you get."

The bear stopped and looked in their direction. He shook his head back and forth, then stood on his back paws. He looked massive. Her body shuddered at the sight. He dropped to all fours, let out a roar and walked toward them.

"If you shoot and miss or wound the bear, he will charge us all and mangle everyone until he falls over dead." Kendall straightened his posture and faced the bear.

Connor stepped beside Kendall and pointed his pistol at the animal.

Kendall shoved Connor's hand in the air and the gun went off. The bear turned and ran into the woods. "What did I just say? It's best to leave him be." Kendall searched for the bear hiding behind the bushes, then continued downhill, taking long strides.

"I ran him off," Connor smarted back at Kendall.

"It could have backfired on you and caused him to charge. Don't be so trigger-happy. You may need those bullets for protection later," Kendall yelled over his shoulder as he proceeded downhill.

Haley hurried to catch up with him. "That was close. Remind me to take up jogging when we get out of here."

Kendall shook his head and gave a short laugh. "I don't think I've ever met anyone like you."

"Is that a good thing or a bad thing?" She waited for an answer.

"It's good." He shot her a glance and smiled. Where did she stand with this handsome firefighter?

After a few minutes of grunts and groans from the group, Kendall paused. The forest thickened and grew darker.

"I can hardly see where I'm going," J.R. said.

"We'll have to press through this thistle patch to reach the boulders and cave on the other side. Be careful and keep your arms in the air." Kendall lifted his arms.

"How come?" Connor's tone was always accusatory or demeaning.

"They have thorns. A lot of thorns, so if you don't want multiple pricks, you'll keep your hands away from them." Kendall shoved a hanging limb aside.

"Can't we go around?" Connor drew a circle in the air with his finger.

"If you see a clear path, then you take over the

lead. Otherwise, we're taking the straight shot before it's totally dark." Irritation rose in Kendall's voice.

Haley pressed her lips together and looked down at her lounge pants. The various plants, foliage and brush around them had already snagged at the legs and they'd merely stopped at the edge of the thistle patch. Bee-like stings threatened her entire body. Being shorter than everyone else made this part of the hike worse. She swallowed and imagined all the pricks that would penetrate her clothes. If Kendall thought this was the best path, who was she to question? She bit the inside of her lip. The idea of feeling a million needles all over, including on her unprotected feet, raised her stress level to the max.

"Go wherever you want. I'm with Kendall." Haley lifted her arms and held Kendall's shirtsleeve. "I'm ready."

Kendall blew out a loud huff. "Ready?"

He hated they'd reached this point, and he didn't enjoy subjecting Haley to such a rigorous, painful journey. His concerns weren't so much with the convicts as they were for her. Maybe he needed a change of attitude and should pray for them, like Haley said. How could he get on the same prayer level as her? He'd missed something in his relationship with God. Whatever it was, he couldn't put a finger on it.

Step by step, he pressed into the weeds. His pants were thicker than Haley's which made it harder for thorns to poke through. He glanced back at her. She'd pasted a grimace on her face. Poor girl. If there were a better route, he'd have taken it.

"Everybody holding up okay?" he asked.

Grumbles, grunts and groans filtered into his ears. Haley hadn't made a sound. Her lips pressed together as she let go of his sleeve and held her arms high. Now and then, he noticed she'd squeeze her eyes closed and push forward as the thorns tugged on her shirt.

The thorny patch thinned out at the edge of tall pine trees. A nice reprieve from the prickly weeds, but the weeds were an instant torch if the blaze reached them. The sun dropped partially behind the mountain and the orange glow of the fire shone in the distance.

"We made it." Kendall stepped on pine needles and turned around to check on everyone. Haley slipped beside him, picking the broken thorns from her clothes. Her T-shirt had tiny bloody spots where thorns pricked her skin. Still, she hadn't complained.

The unhappy men caught up with them. "Don't take us through something like that again." J.R. picked at his jeans. "You did that on purpose."

"Yeah. Do it again and you'll wish you hadn't," Connor said.

"Aha. Much better." Blake stretched his arms out under the pine trees, still hanging on to Kendall's tool. "Easier walking, too."

"Not so easy." Haley started into the pine forest. "There are protruding tree roots, fallen trees, uneven ground with a lot of places to sprain an ankle."

"She's right." Kendall winked at her. She caught on quick.

"It's better than what we just went through. Where's that cabin? It's gettin' darker, and I need some shuteye." Mac pushed his sleeves up and slapped at his pants. "Felt like something was crawling up my leg." He jumped back and yelled, slapping wildly at his thigh. "Get it off."

A large hairy spider didn't want to let go. Blake eased the Pulaski across Mac's pants and knocked it to the ground. "Was that a tarantula?"

"Not here in the Blue Ridge Mountains." Kendall eyed Mac. "It's what we call a trapdoor spider, which is like the tarantula. It's not poisonous, so its bite won't kill you. Might ache a little."

"Who would've thought a tough guy like you would be afraid of spiders?" Connor chided.

"I'm not. That thing was a dinosaur." Mac shook his leg and looked at the back of his pants. "Are there any more on me? Where's our cabin?"

"It's not a cabin. The terrain gets rougher the closer we get to the rock formations and the cave." Kendall eyed Haley. "Watch your step. You're doing great."

"I've got this. I think." She pushed her long hair behind her ears.

They trekked through the pine needles, stepped on and over fallen trees. The smoke wasn't so bad down in the valley, but that wouldn't last long if the upper-level turbulence shifted and changed wind direction. Kendall looked back at the fire on three sides of them. His stomach churned and growled. Yep, he was hungry, but he was more concerned about all the pine trees and dried needles going up in flames.

With the cave in sight, Kendall looked around for the bear they'd seen earlier. Would they be invading the bear's sleeping quarters? Not a fight he cared to encounter.

"Look, I think I see it." Mac laughed as though he'd conquered some impressive feat.

"They haven't found us yet. We're on the road to true freedom." Connor rushed to the cave entrance and stopped.

Kendall approached and lowered his pack, reaching inside.

Suddenly, three of the men surrounded him with their pistols pointed at him. "You'd better remove your hand slowly. No sudden moves." J.R. pushed the pistol into Kendall's temple.

Kendall threw his hands in the air. His heart pounded in his throat. It was bad enough to have one weapon pointed in his face, but three? "I was reaching for my flashlight." Kendall reached in and pulled out his flashlight. "I was going to check and make sure that bear wasn't inside before we try sharing space. I don't think the bear would be very welcoming." He held the flashlight in the air until the guys tucked their weapons back into their waistbands. "You're too suspicious and jumpy. Do you really think I'd try something with all of you packing heat?"

"Thanks, Kendall. You're constantly watching

out for everyone, and they have no appreciation at all." Haley pursed her lips at Blake. An expression Kendall guessed Blake understood.

Kendall swallowed what little saliva he had in his parched mouth at the thought of entering an inky cave in the dark. Not good conditions for mere men searching for a place to stay until daylight. A bear could already be asleep or could mosey in during the night. Somebody would have to stand watch.

He popped his neck and stepped cautiously into the coolness of the cave, shining the light in every direction. Claw marks decorated the stone walls, a pile of dried bear scat lay beside some gnarly bones and bear tracks were in the dirt. Dried leaves and a few twigs blown in by the wind piled up along the knobby stone walls.

His pulse throbbed in his neck. Would his light find the eyes of a bear or coyote, or even a rattle-snake curled in a dark cubby? No heavy breathing or growling, but that didn't mean the bear wouldn't return to his haven. The stale air mixed with smoke curled his nose. He'd smelled worse.

God, could You keep us safe in here, so we have a cool place to rest?

If they weren't in such a precarious situation and it wasn't dark already, he'd opt to keep moving. Haley stood at the opening of the cave, peering inside while he'd checked things out. He stopped in front of Haley and pushed the hair from her face with his finger. Her eyes met his and for a moment his heart picked up speed. An unexpected urge to kiss her right there in the dark almost got the best of him. Had she sensed the almost romantic moment?

She opened her mouth to say something, but closed it and pressed her lips together.

"It's safe." His soft words came out in a whisper to Haley. She smiled the first genuine smile he'd seen all day. He suddenly felt energized.

He stuck his head out and announced the cave was clear. The fearless, tough men stood back, almost at the tree line, holding their guns again. Blake leaned on Kendall's tool like it was a walking stick. Kendall shook his head. At least he hadn't tossed it aside. They would need it later.

"Well." Connor spoke up in his unpleasant tone. "What are we waiting for?"

"There are signs a bear has been here, so grab a few pieces of firewood. We'll build a small fire at the opening of the cave to discourage its return or other unwanted guests." Kendall stepped back inside the cave.

Blake's voice drifted inside. "You get the wood. We're not taking orders from you. We are in control here."

"Just get a stick. They're outnumbered. They ain't going nowhere." Mac tossed a few small branches toward the mouth of the cave, then stepped inside. "Thought it would smell fresher than this." He sniffed as he moseyed in deeper.

Behind him, Connor, Blake and J.R. entered and dropped more broken limbs in the pile.

"Could've been worse." J.R. rubbed his hand over

the claw marks on the stone wall. "Hope he's found a new home."

"Seems kinda ironic that we're running from a fire and yet we're starting a fire." Connor plopped down on the ground and brushed the dried leaves to the side. "At least it is cool in here. Man, my legs are tired."

"Mine, too." Mac stretched his legs out and rubbed his thighs. "Those thorns didn't help matters any, and I hope I never see a spider like that again. I'm staying as far away from the mountains as I can when I get out of here."

"You've got that right." J.R. untied his shoe and rubbed his foot.

Kendall listened to the irresponsible men whine. Haley helped him build the fire, then scooted back and leaned against the bumpy cave wall. He sat beside her, glad for the temporary relief from the elements and the wildfire.

He set his pack beside him and leaned back. Silence only lasted a moment as they all looked at each other.

"You got anything to eat or drink in that bag?" Connor jerked it from Kendall's grip. He tossed everything out on the ground, including the three orange jumpsuits and Kendall's folding rake and folding shovel. A few granola bars, protein bars, six single packs of beef jerky and his water thermos scattered on the cave floor.

"Ah, look what we've got here." He grabbed one of the beef jerkies and ripped it open, tossed the paper on the ground and took a big bite. "Why do you have those jumpsuits? We ain't wearing them again."

"I'm turning them in to the authorities." Kendall's response had them all looking at him.

"No, you're not." Mac grabbed them and tossed them in the fire. Smoke filtered through the cave and the flame intensified, blocking the exit. "Guess no varmints will walk through that fire." He coughed as he laughed.

"What did you do that for?" Blake fanned the smoke from his face. "Now you've got it hot in here."

"Give me one of those." Mac reached for a beef jerky. Connor tossed J.R. and Blake one each. "Who eats granola? That's all grain like you'd give animals."

"I'll have a granola bar." Haley reached for one and cut her eyes over at Mac.

Kendall's insides boiled. He picked up all the trash, scooped up a granola bar and handed it to her. "Guess I'll have the protein bar." He took the forty-two-ounce thermos and offered Haley a drink first. He managed a couple of swigs before J.R. took the thermos from him and guzzled several swallows.

Blake snatched the thermos from J.R. "Not too much, man, this has got to do us until we're out of here."

Did these guys ever stop complaining? How did they agree on an escape plan? Kendall waited for the fire to die down before he leaned toward the cave opening to check on the orange sky. Smoke swirled outside. Small amounts of smoke blew inside their shelter, but it hadn't affected their breathing any more than Mac's stunt with the jumpsuits had. He sat back down beside Haley.

Kendall took a small stick and drew in the dirt on the floor. "Who was the mastermind in your escape?"

All four men stopped what they were doing and looked up at him like he had four heads. He figured they'd tell him it was none of his business, but they started laughing. Kendall didn't see anything funny about his question. Haley shrugged her shoulders. At least she wasn't laughing. In fact, she looked disgusted with them.

Blake held the remaining bite of his jerky up like it was a toast. The others did a fist bump. "I planned the whole thing. Took Mac and Connor a few days to come to their senses and join the plan. After some convincing, J.R. liked the challenge and was all in."

"Yeah." Mac pushed J.R.'s shoulder. "It took J.R. a few days to see the benefits of doing something daring and spicing up his life. Told him I had money stashed from the banks I'd robbed, and I'd give him enough to get reestablished across the border. I'd even let him work with me if he wanted."

"We hid out in the bathroom and waited until lockdown, then after J.R. turned in the count for the night, he took us through the back way and showed us the best route to take to get through the prison yard unnoticed," Blake said.

Connor pulled his pistol out. "Yep. He hid these guns out by the dumpster. We grabbed them and ran to the fence where J.R. told us erosion had caused a hole by the drainage ditch behind the chow hall. An area where inmates weren't allowed to go. We crawled through and jumped in an old truck J.R. got at a junk yard under a fake name."

"That piece of junk broke down on us at the entrance of the resort." Blake took the last bite of his beef jerky. "Where else could we go, but searching for a cabin to hide in?"

J.R. scooted back and rested against the wall. "After they made it sound so challenging, I volunteered to do rounds in their cell house, and I altered the inmate count." His belly shook with laughter. "No one knew these guys were missing until the next morning when I was changing shift. Most excitement I've had in years. Oh, the guns I supplied, I bought them off the street."

Kendall shook his head at the gloating these guys did, sharing their successful escape plan. He caught a glance of Haley watching him. What was she thinking? Was she still wondering if he believed her story? Would these escapees kill them, or would any of them live long enough to be rescued?

Chapter Six

Haley couldn't help herself. Kendall differed from any man she'd ever met. He'd been a shoulder to lean on through the complete nightmare. She was also reminded of a verse in Proverbs that described the name of the Lord as a Strong Tower. That verse also said, "The righteous run to it and are safe." Between the strength of the Lord and Kendall by her side, she was going to make it through this.

Lord, keep us safe, please.

Blake and his friends acted as though they didn't have a care in the world, which seemed to irritate Kendall, and she didn't blame him. They were constantly belittling and questioning his professional knowledge. Were they really that oblivious to reality?

The convicts butted heads several times, so it appeared there was no true respect for one another. Everyone had their own agenda. And to think, Blake admitted to being the ringleader of their escape. He'd be in more trouble than the others when the authorities caught up with them.

Smoke boiled inside the cave and rolled back out. Everyone covered their mouths and coughed. Kendall covered his nose and mouth and went to the opening of the cave. He leaned outside, then stepped back.

"Just a wind gust." He returned to his seat next to her, took his gloves off for the first time and put his arm around her shoulders. "Get some rest while you can."

She didn't feel so alone with him by her side. She noticed that his left hand had no signs of a ring. No indention, tan line, nothing. He'd been truthful. A trait that made her like him even more. Would she feel differently once they were out of danger, or had she subconsciously accepted this brave firefighter? Her emotions played havoc in her evaluation of him in this dangerous setting. If given a choice right now, she'd allow him into her life once the rescue team found them.

She yawned and laid her head on his shoulder.

"Hey, fire boy, quit hitting on my cousin." Blake leaned toward her.

Haley lifted her head and glanced at Kendall. His lips tightened. "Mind your own business, Blake. I haven't forgotten that you left me in that cabin to burn alive. Why would you even put yourself in this situation? Don't you and your friends want a life you don't have to run from?"

Her disappointment at Blake's poor decisions

threatened tears. She pushed them back, knowing these guys would tease her and accuse her of being weak. Blake and she had so much fun growing up together. She never imagined he'd get caught up in a life of crime. Their dads were brothers and their families always had Sunday dinners together after church. In fact, their homes were on the same block, which made it easy for her and Blake to ride bikes together around the neighborhood, build forts and play kickball with their friends.

She never understood why Blake's dad always brought a bottle of alcohol to their dinners. By the time the meal was over, his speech slurred, and he became angry. Blake and she would slip from the house and run to the wooded lot at the end of the street and swing on grapevines. Then, Blake would throw rocks at a tree and grumble about his dad while she drew circles in the dirt with a stick. She was worried for her cousin, but she didn't know how to help him.

Blake lowered his brows but didn't answer her question. Had she spotted flashes of regret in his eyes? He leaned back and placed his arms across his chest. His friends were already snoring. She laid her head back on Kendall's shoulder again and closed her eyes. Finally, a moment of peace with the roar of the fire in the distance. Who could really sleep when their lives were on the line?

"Is this cave really safe?" Haley's eyes popped open. She examined the rock walls.

His shoulder muscle tensed under her head. When

he didn't answer, she looked at him, noting his lowered brows with an angry look on his face. What did she say wrong?

"Do you honestly think I'd risk lives, including mine, if it weren't?" He didn't look at her.

She leaned away from him. "That's not what I meant."

"You, out of all these guys, should know I wouldn't put any of you in harm's way. It's my job to fight fires and protect." His voice lifted an octave.

"Hey, man, watch your tone." Blake jumped to his feet.

Kendall stood. "Oh, you care about her now?"

J.R. pushed Blake back and rushed into Kendall's face. "Watch your mouth, fire boy." He punched his finger in Kendall's chest.

Kendall shoved J.R. "Who are you calling a boy?" His face turned red.

"Please stop. Arguing isn't getting us anywhere." Haley stepped between Kendall and J.R. "We're all exhausted, and we need our rest. Forget I asked about the cave."

Kendall held his fists up, ready for another attack. Haley placed her hand on his arm and pushed his hands down to his sides. "Forget I said anything."

Connor spat on the ground. "I thought it was an excellent question. Notice he hasn't given us a proper explanation why we stopped here with that blaze waiting to devour us."

"I said stop." Haley gave him as hard a glare as she knew how. "You guys were griping and complaining about being tired. If you didn't want to stop, you should've said something. Besides, you're running away from your responsibilities, trying to escape punishment for the crimes you committed. Kendall runs into the danger zone. He is to be admired for his commitment to help preserve the land and rescue people rather than kill and destroy. At least he does something respectable, unlike you guys."

She reeled in her exasperation with the grumbling men and softened her tone. "You should've noticed by now that Kendall is trying to save us." Smoke forced her to cough. "But, just in case the fire picks up speed, I'll be the first to say I forgive all of you for ruining my vacation, threatening my life and for whatever else you've done, because that's what God would want me to do." She turned to Kendall. "Thank you for putting your life on the line for us."

J.R. fumbled with his backpack, then chimed in with his sarcasm. "God's done nothing for me. Who are you to preach to any of us? You need to shut your mouth before I make you."

"Cool it, man." Blake rubbed his forehead.

"Don't tell us what to do," Mac said.

"Y'all snap at each other like a pack of angry dogs. Evidently, God *is* helping you because you're still alive in this raging wildfire. You might even get to live longer if you turn yourself in to the police." She sat on the cool dirt floor beside Kendall. He hadn't opened his mouth since the outburst. Maybe she should follow suit once again and keep quiet.

She studied each of the men as they settled back

and snored within minutes. In her wariness, she sensed an overwhelming concern for them. They had families, too. Parents, wives, girlfriends, siblings and possibly kids. They must be devastated over their incarcerated loved ones' poor choices in life.

Lord, please rescue us. All of us. And help them see You are the answer to their problems.

Kendall mentioned he compared God to his dad, who judged him and believed he could do nothing right. Her heart broke over this perception of a heavenly Father. Rejection was bad enough when it came from friends and even coworkers, but for a parent to turn away from their child had devastating and long-lasting effects.

She'd experienced betrayal and disappointment in her past relationship, but that wasn't nearly as bad as what Kendall must have gone through with his father.

Her stomach still churned over being gullible and believing her now-ex was single. His lies and betrayal cut deep. But even that pain could never measure up to the disapproval expressed by Kendall's dad over his career choice. Regardless of age, there's nothing more encouraging on this earth than having a parent's blessing.

She picked at a hangnail. Kendall wasn't as much of a stranger now that they'd been side by side for the last two days, and now going into the second night. He was a respectable person. If only there was something she could do to reunite him with his dad. Prayer was her only option.

Lord, You are always faithful and I'm striving to

do better. Please help Kendall reestablish a relationship with You and with his dad.

If only her thoughts would shut down and she could sleep. Her body ached for a nap, but rest evaded her. Kendall's head turned toward her. She was certain he'd lightly pressed his cheek against her head before moving it again. She pretended to be asleep, but his expression of tenderness warmed her heart.

Kendall's light touches on her shoulder where he'd put his arm around her let her know he wasn't sleeping. If she'd learned anything about him, it was that he would give up everything to save her and the escapees. Such a commitment and confirmation of his integrity.

The roar of the fire sounded distant inside the cave, like the constant hum of the fan in her grandmother's window.

"I shouldn't have been so presumptuous, thinking you were questioning my judgment. I make mistakes, too," Kendall whispered in her ear.

"Forget it. We're all on edge. I don't know about those guys, but you and I needed a break."

"No argument there. How are you holding up?" he asked.

"I've been better, but I'm alive, so all is well." Her body stung where all those thorns pricked her skin, her feet throbbed from improper mountain climbing shoes and her head still hurt from falling in the cabin. She could go on with a list, but what good would it do?

"You're handling things like a champ." His fingers patted her shoulder.

What could she say? Determination drove her forward. His constant reassurance that they'd make it to safety played a big part in her not giving up.

"Is the fire's roar always that loud?"

"Pretty much. As long as the wind doesn't shift again, we have a brief window of rest." He leaned forward and tossed a couple of small branches into the fire. "We'll have to hit it hard at dawn to get out of this burning 'U' zone before it traps us. Makes me a little nervous that we've stayed in one place so long. This forest is too dangerous to tackle a wildfire in the dark."

She yawned. Her body relaxed and her eyelids grew heavy. His voice faded into a distant tunnel. Silence.

What seemed like a minute must have been hours before a dim light filtered into the cave. She opened her eyes. Morning had arrived and that meant more hiking on her sore feet.

Lord, send help to us today, please.

"Got to go. Everyone up." Kendall tapped her shoulder. "We've got to get out of here."

She jumped at the urgency of his voice. A deafening roar filled with snapping, sizzling and popping attacked her ears. Goose bumps raced over her sweaty body. The cave had turned into an oven. Her clothes were soaked with perspiration.

Kendall kicked dirt over their small cave fire. Why? Habit? With the blaze on top of them, that campfire looked trivial. The wildfire flames seemed to know they were hiding out. Red and orange streaks reached into the cave and withdrew as the outside turbulence stirred. The rock formation on the ceiling cracked.

"Thought this was a safe place." Mac hopped to his feet, wiping his brow.

"It was, but evidently the wind shifted while we were sleeping." Kendall reached for Haley and took her hand in his. "Run out and to your left, away from the fire. It's literally on top of the cave. If you turn right, you'll run into the flames."

"Don't have to tell me twice." Blake darted out of the cave before anyone else, followed by his three friends.

"Let's go." Haley squeezed his hand. "Whatever happens, I trust you."

Kendall held Haley's hand as they ducked and ran out of the cave together. Intense heat slapped them in the face as flames taunted them. Thick smoke hung in the air. He held the collar of his shirt over his mouth. Haley did likewise with the bandanna he'd given her. Smart girl. Fast learner and brave, too.

They ran several yards before Kendall stopped. The area was narrow, but if he dug a fire line, it might slow the advancement of the fire and allow them time to get farther away.

"Blake, toss me that Pulaski. I need to dig a fire line." Kendall held his hand out.

Blake hesitated before handing the tool over. "Give it back when you're done."

"You could help." Kendall shot a glance at the other guys while he pulled out his folding shovel and rake.

"I'll take one." Haley stepped forward. "Tell me what to do."

Kendall handed Haley the rake and tossed the shovel at Blake. "Start clearing the grass away and leave a line of dirt."

"Does this really do any good?" Connor spoke up, digging the heel of his shoe into the ground.

"It does when I'm with my handcrew. All we can do is try before we make a run for it." Kendall pounded the ground with his Pulaski as hard and as fast as he could. "With my team, we normally dig a timber fire line about twenty to thirty feet wide with a three-to-four-foot scrape."

Haley went right to work and scraped the ground alongside him. Blake fell in beside her and began digging. Mac picked up a large stick while Connor and J.R. dug down with their heels. Teamwork. Even criminals knew how to get along when conditions were right.

Trees burst into flames too close for comfort. Kendall backed away. "The fire's moving too fast. Let's go. Cover your mouths as best as you can." He took the tools and stuffed them in his pack as he jogged away from danger. "Blake, here." He tossed the Pulaski as Blake had requested earlier.

Haley's sandals inhibited her fast pace. He monitored her in case she started falling behind. The smoke grew thicker, and the wind gusts made it difficult to catch a good breath. In fact, the smoke was so thick he couldn't see anyone, not even Haley. He reached his hand out in search of her. She wasn't beside him. The roar rumbled so loud he couldn't hear if she screamed.

All he could do was keep running as straight forward as the rough ground allowed. Another gust swirled, making the smoke thinner. His stomach plummeted. Right before him was a steep incline filled with a mossy grass-like foliage and seedling trees. He'd experienced this type of groundcover before. It softened the earth and gave way easily, like climbing in mud. Not enough to hold on to.

There was no other way around, only upward. A sultry breeze thinned the smoke, and he spotted everyone. They were all accounted for. Haley crawled on her hands and knees up the incline. The inmates scampered upward as fast as they could but with nothing to hold on to except for the moss, they slid down several feet with their hands full of the green foliage.

Mac held on to a small tree and repositioned his footing, pushing himself up a few more feet. Blake slammed the Pulaski into the ground and pulled himself up little by little. Connor and J.R. developed their own techniques as they inched up the slick mountain. They held short sticks in both hands and jabbed them in the ground with each step.

Kendall dug his fingers into the soft ground,

rammed the toe of his boot into the dirt and pulled himself up. The sandals weren't working well for Haley. She reached for a seedling tree, and it pulled up from the soil. She slid halfway down from where she'd started.

Between the unstable wind conditions, the continuous roar of the fire and the growing heat intensity, Kendall reasoned he must rescue Haley if she was going to make it over this normally beautiful mountain. He moved sideways, with his boots shoved into the ground, until he stood by her side.

Her eyes met with his and her fear pricked his heart. He dug the toe of his boot into the dirt and put his arm around her waist. She latched onto him as though her life depended on it, and it did. He pointed to the base of the small trees.

"Hold on here, but don't pull hard. Let your feet dig into the ground, then push up. You can do this, Haley." Kendall helped balance her and kept her from sliding.

"I… I'm trying." Her voice staggered.

"Look at me." He pointed two fingers at her, then back at himself. "Calm down and focus. You're panicking and it's fighting against you. Focus."

She shook her head, still holding on to him with a firm grip.

"Step with me. Ready? One, two, three, step." Kendall held on to her while he searched for something stable. Through the thin swirls of smoke, a large tree several feet up came into view. If he could reach his rope, maybe he could get it around the tree and pull her up.

He retrieved the rope from his fire pack. The challenge of holding on to Haley and tossing a rope wasn't going to work. He needed an extra set of hands. A tree popped, cracked and sizzled, then fell beside them. They had to get up this mountain if they were going to make it.

"Throw it to me," Blake yelled from above the large tree.

Relief settled Kendall's soaring thoughts. He tossed the rope as best as he could. It fell short. Amazingly, J.R., Connor, Mac and Blake formed a human chain and stretched far enough to grab Kendall's rope. They worked at record speed, tying it to the large tree and tossing it down to them.

Kendall wrapped it around the two of them and the escapees pulled them to the top.

"Great job, guys." Kendall untied the rope and rolled it up.

"I thought I'd lost everyone." Haley tugged at her hair. "The smoke is so thick and stifling. Thank you for saving me." She hugged Blake and reached for his friends. They backed away and held their hands up.

"I'm good. No hugging necessary." Connor backed away.

"Me, too." Mac held his head back.

Relief washed over Kendall. Who knew these tough guys would rescue the very ones they'd threatened to kill? The joy on Haley's face was all he needed to keep going.

She turned to him. He lifted his eyebrows. "I'll take a hug."

Haley leaned into his arms and held on tight. He squeezed her slight frame. If only he could hold her longer.

"Thank you for coming back for me. I couldn't get a foothold."

"I'd never leave you behind. You can count on it." He gave her hand a light squeeze. The swoosh and popping alerted him that another flaming tree had fallen against the incline, which meant the mountainside would burn in a matter of seconds. The unstable wind conditions picked up and more smoke came after them.

"Come on. Let's get out of here." Kendall tightened his grip on Haley's hand. Her tangled hair hung over her face. She had a right to be afraid. He was, too, but he wasn't about to admit it right now. She needed encouragement, and he'd give it to her.

Kendall paused and observed the forest below from the top of the small mountain they'd climbed. At least the blaze hadn't closed them in. The threat was still there, so they had to keep moving until he could find another place for them to catch a breather.

"Now what kind of challenge are you going to get us into, fire boy?" J.R. picked up a long stick and stabbed it into the ground. "Think I'll hang on to this."

Kendall cringed. He wasn't fond of the name-calling, but he guessed it could be worse. J.R. hadn't come across as being sarcastic. Maybe he was calming down, knowing Kendall wasn't trying to get away or put them in danger. He had no idea what was going through J.R.'s head.

The roar of an airplane sounded.

"What's that?" Haley asked.

Everyone fixed their eyes on Kendall. "It's the airplane most likely carrying smoke jumpers. They're trained in wildland fires." He stretched his arm out and pointed toward the outline of the fire. "Firefighters will jump from the plane along the edge of the fire. They're still a distance away, so we aren't out of the woods yet, no pun intended."

"Don't you go pulling any tricks on us." Connor stiffened.

"Do I look like I want to pull any pranks right now?" Kendall stood his ground. "The good news is fire moves slower downhill, so we'll have a bit of a reprieve, but can't take it for granted. Flames can pop up anywhere. With all the floating embers, we're at risk of being blocked in."

Mac stabbed his stick in the ground again. "You encourage us, you knock us down again. I'm not so sure you know what you're talking about."

Kendall pressed his lips together. All the times he'd fought wildfires, he'd run toward the fire many times, and rarely away from it. His present situation stretched his firefighting training and experience. Time to draw from the well of what-ifs and pray for wisdom and direction.

Don't let the fire close us in. I'm trusting You.

Chapter Seven

Haley couldn't believe her eyes. The magnitude of a wildfire was far more than she'd ever imagined. She twisted her long, tangled hair and formed a ball on top of her head. With all the trees and bushes constantly raking against her, the long strands would be back on her shoulders in a few minutes.

She'd grown fond of her new firefighter friend. The bravery and selflessness he consistently showed, knowing the escapees threatened to kill them. He'd still fought to get them to safety, too.

Blake had grown silent. Was he rethinking his actions? She couldn't decide about the others since she'd only just met them, after they'd forced themselves into her life. If given the chance, she might ask about their families. They were a moody bunch.

Kendall's hand wrapped around hers like it was meant to be there. She'd held his hand for most of the past two and a half days and hers fit in his perfectly. His dirty face had a few dark streaks. Her face probably matched his, except for the stubby beard forming. She licked her lips. *Yuck!* Dirt and grime hit her taste buds. She spat and resolved not to do that again. She stepped over a large tree root and tugged at her foot, stuck in a vine.

"Hold on, a vine got caught in between my foot and the sandal." She leaned against Kendall, broke the vine and tore it away. "Okay, I'm good. The fire's roar doesn't seem so loud now."

"The blaze is back over the mountain, but don't let that fool you. The fires east and west of us are crawling inward. At some point, the blaze we left behind will top the mountain, then the chase is on again." Kendall held a limb back from smacking her face.

She grabbed the branch and held it until she'd passed it. "Tell me something about yourself."

"Like what?" He glanced her direction. "I've been studying for a promotion, but I had to get my bachelor's degree before I could qualify for a GS5 ground-level forestry position. I took the online test the night before I found you in the cabin. Don't know yet if I passed. What about you?"

"Hey, fire boy." J.R. high-stepped over some tall weeds. "Are you leading us straight into the hands of the law?"

"How many times do I have to tell you I'm trying to get us out of the forest alive, even if it means we run into a rural road, a train track, another river or meet up with other firefighters?" Kendall's voice held patience. "I have no other agenda."

"What's that roaring? It sounds different from the fire," Haley said.

Kendall stopped, then started walking again. "If I'm not mistaken, it's a waterfall."

Haley spun at the movement off to her left. She tugged on Kendall's shirt. "I saw something move over there. I think it was an animal. Looked like a dog."

"Probably a coyote." Kendall helped her over a small dip in the terrain. "Nothing to worry about. They don't normally attack people. Besides, he's probably trying to find a safe place like us."

Haley pursed her lips. *Don't worry?* She didn't run into wild animals back home. Not that she was against them or fearful. She just didn't know enough about their behaviors to be comfortable with sightings out in the forest. The zoo was more her style.

"Hey." Kendall tugged on her arm. "I'm serious. Don't dwell on his presence. There's probably a bear or two around, plus a few deer. They are all aware of pending danger."

The downhill slope deepened. Haley had to lean back to keep from tumbling forward. The guys followed suit, but they took faster, longer strides the steeper the terrain got. Her foot slipped on a rock.

"Ouch." Her ankle stung. "Almost twisted my ankle." She wasn't admitting to the pain unless she couldn't walk. She'd suck it up and try to be as strong as these men.

"Sure you're okay?" Kendall bent over and rubbed her sock-covered ankle.

She pulled her foot away. "Positive." She started walking again and her foot almost slipped, but she caught herself.

Kendall's steps appeared sure and steady. Proof he'd walked the mountains before and had trained for much of what they'd encountered. They came to a sudden halt. The decline ended at a small cliff, or to her, it looked like a steep drop-off. Blake, Connor, Mac and J.R. stood at the bottom and waited for them.

"Thought the firefighter could walk faster than that." Blake stood with his hands on his hips.

"I'm the one holding things up." Haley didn't want them harassing Kendall when it was her fault they weren't moving as fast as they should. "These sandals aren't made for mountain climbing."

"Why didn't you get your shoes?" Mac chimed in with his hands in his pockets.

"You can't be serious." She squinted at Blake. "You left me behind, remember?"

Blake wiped his mouth with his hand. His eyes briefly met her eyes before he looked away. No retort. Was he having second thoughts about his actions?

Kendall sat at the edge of the small ravine and hopped off. He turned to her and held his arms out. "Jump."

If she stalled, they'd blame her for keeping them back while the fire approached. She wouldn't give them any more reason to taunt her. She squatted like Kendall had and pushed from the cliff, landing partly in his arms and partly with her feet on the ground. A soft landing, thanks to him.

In the distance, fire shot from both sides of the forest as though the wind invited it to show a destructive flame dance. Lightning flashed across the sky. Behind them, fire fingers pushed Haley and the others closer to the dance floor.

"Was that lightning? Is it going to rain?" Haley forced herself to remain calm and positive.

Lord, I don't see a way out of here, but You do.

"Not hardly. Firestorms can develop their own lightning." Kendall wiped his hands on his pants and took her hand in his.

Straight in front of them was a valley full of tall, dried grass that tossed with the warm breeze. Smoke dipped down and swirled back up in a teasing manner. She took in a fresh breath before it returned and stifled the air again.

"Why can't your handcrew team meet us in this area?" Haley studied their position. They'd made it this far and survived more than she thought. Surely there's help somewhere close.

"Can't speak for the crew, but I'm certain they have evaluated the situation, studied the fire perimeters, the weather and the wind. Fire makes its own wind, so we're not dealing fully with the atmospheric pressure and natural winds from everyday weather. We've changed directions multiple times, so they don't know exactly where we are, only that we're running away from the blaze." Kendall dropped her hand. "Once we're on the other side of this meadow, we will take a break and grab a sip of the remaining water."

The inmates high-stepped it ahead of them and left Kendall and her pulling up the rear. Haley walked sure-footed through the tall grass. Leaves mixed with occasional embers tossed through the air. She kept watch and made sure the embers didn't land on her clothes or skin.

The ground wasn't exactly level. They'd survived worse. Her legs still ached and her sore muscles rebelled from all the climbing and running. Not to mention her feet suffered a lot of abuse. Breathing wasn't the easiest, either, with the altitude and all the smoke stirring. There was no other choice but to press forward.

Kendall stayed with her all the way across the meadow back into a dense forest. She'd grown comfortable with him by her side.

"Tell me." Kendall changed the subject. "Where do you work?"

She let out a chuckle. "I was a dental hygienist until I arrived at the office a couple of weeks ago only to find a note posted on the door. *No Longer in Business.* For the time being, I'm unemployed."

They caught up with the four inmates. Funny how they ran ahead of them, leaving their hostages behind.

"What type of business shuts down without notifying their employees first?" Kendall asked as they caught up with the guys.

"Exactly the question I had." Haley sat on a log

while Kendall pulled out his thermos. He'd suggested water. No way was she going to pass up a drink. Drinking liquids in high altitudes was supposed to help avoid altitude sickness and dehydration. So far, she'd made it okay.

"You stick your hands in people's mouths all day and breathe their breath with all those germs?" Connor plopped down and leaned against a tree. "I don't get how people can do that."

"For your information, I wear gloves and a mask." Haley refused to try explaining her career to a convict. Wasn't worth the argument. "If you've ever had a toothache, I'm sure you were more than happy to open your mouth at the dentist's office."

She continued, "I'm thinking about relocating to a smaller town and looking for a job."

Blake groaned. "You can hide better in big cities."

"I have nothing or no one to hide from," Haley said.

"You won't be going anywhere." Mac, who leaned against a rock, straightened. "This forest is as far as you and Mr. Firefighter go. We have to make a clean break."

Kendall nosed up to Mac. "By now the ranger station, fire department and police department know all of you are with us. Regardless of what you do, you've already made things worse for yourselves by escaping. Adding other charges like holding hostages will get you a longer sentence. Is that what you want?"

Haley waited for a fight to break out. Kendall backed down and returned to her side. The men's silence meant one of two things. Either they'd let Kendall and her go, or they'd already agreed, regardless of the situation, they'd eliminate them when the timing was right.

Kendall's parched throat longed for more water. He refused to take more than a couple of swallows from his thermos and would limit everyone else's intake. Not many bars were left either. Once they were gone, they'd be at the mercy of the forest for whatever hydration and nourishment they could find.

His thoughts drifted to his handcrew team, who were undoubtedly out there, frantically working to contain the fire and find him. The smoke jumpers had already hit the ground somewhere in the distance. What seemed like a straightforward path in their direction could be a death trap. Plus, with the erratic behavior of the wildfire, his radio demolished and his cell phone dead, no one knew their location.

The teams were privy to weather updates and the perimeters and behaviors of the fire. He trusted his team and wouldn't doubt their motives or decisions. Kendall decided, as weary and hungry as he was, he must remain alert and follow through with his evacuation plan for these people. Now, he was making judgment calls with each shift of the wind.

He analyzed their location and wiped his brow with his sleeve. If there wasn't a firestorm, the mountain range would be chilly, consistent with October temperatures. However, the fiery blaze had warmed the forest up considerably. Dark gray boiling smoke billowed overhead, and temperatures teetered around ninety-five sitting in the shade. Much more heat intensity would make them at risk of heat strokes.

Had his dad heard he'd rescued a woman and met up with three escapees and a rogue prison guard? Deep down, Kendall knew his dad loved him, but he'd barely spoken to Kendall in the past four years. The disappointment cut deep, and yet he longed to restore their relationship. Would this dangerous situation cause his dad to reconsider and be happy for him?

His dad's welding business was a thriving business, but it just wasn't the job he'd wanted. Working as a Forest Service firefighter was a dream come true and one he intended to stay with. This is where he wanted to be. Well, not lost in the woods amid a firestorm, but as a career.

"Kendall." Haley's voice pulled his thoughts back to the present. "Looks like some dead trees lying on the ground over there." She pointed ahead of them, off to the right. "Think we could stop there for a bit?"

He turned around to check the status of the fire. He'd rather get farther away. Blake and his friends had already spotted the area Haley mentioned and headed that way. He guessed it wouldn't hurt.

"Maybe for a minute. By the looks of that fire, we're not gaining any ground. It's steadily narrowing the gap between us." He rubbed the back of his neck while tension tugged at his stomach.

Even his unwanted guests looked rather frayed. The lack of proper fluids and nourishment showed on their faces. He didn't need a mirror to see the distress on his face. His neck and shoulders held more tension than he'd ever expected to encounter.

Haley was to be admired for her bravery. Being from the city hadn't hindered her ability to keep up, for the most part. She had a confidence about her that drew him closer. She'd probably never want to wear another pair of sandals. He could only guess how bruised and sore her feet were. His feet ached, and he had on proper boots for the rough terrain.

They reached the end of the short meadow. Kendall tossed out snacks for everyone. He stared into the forest. It appeared thicker than the last densely populated area they'd emerged from. Not a beneficial situation. Amid the pine, oak and maple trees, the undergrowth held vines, shrubs, poison ivy and wild ferns, making the mountain prime kindling for a raging wildfire. Rockslides were another threatening possibility. They may have to find refuge among the boulders again or find another river. His lack of satisfactory choices made him uneasy.

"Where do we go from here, fire boy?" J.R. chomped on his beef jerky.

Kendall retrieved his map. He still refused to acknowledge J.R.'s name-calling. The man did it on purpose because he knew it agitated him. He unfolded the map, turned it right side up, slid his finger over the mountain range and pointed. He spun, checked the layout and rechecked the map. His shoulders dropped and the hair on the back of his neck bristled. If he figured accurately, they were smack in the middle of the mountain range, where the slopes and ravines scattered in unexplained formations. That meant more climbing once they reached the bottom.

He spread the map out on a log where black ants rushed about their business. "If you really want to know—" he pointed to the center of the map "—we are right about here."

Everyone gathered around him and groaned. His sentiments exactly.

Haley stepped back, wide-eyed. "Seriously?"

What could he say to bring confidence? They were still alive, so he'd kept them safe this far. All he could do was to offer his best. He wanted to go home, too.

Connor shoved the map off the log, tearing part of it. "What do you know? You're probably telling us that so we'll traipse off in another direction while you and Haley escape by a shorter route. Well, I'm not buying it."

"We're sticking together," Blake said. "Kendall has more experience than any of us. You know that. He wants out of here, too."

"Who said he and Haley were going free?" Mac straightened, rolled his shoulders and popped his neck. "We haven't agreed to let them go."

Blake threw his hand in the air. "Drop it, Mac, and the rest of you. We won't gain anything by knocking them off. Get over it and let's just get out of here."

Kendall observed their body language while he became increasingly frustrated. He would stomp and

Loretta Eidson   123

pitch a fit if it would help. Not here, not now, never. Acting foolish only lessened alertness. Enough of that. A minute was up. They had to get going. He folded the torn map and placed it back inside his pack.

"Let's go see if we can find smoke-free air." Kendall led the group forward.

"I'm ready for fresh air."

"Me, too, but there's nothing you can do about the smoke right now." Connor tossed a small branch aside and walked into the woods.

"I'm just glad we're able to breathe, even if it is a little smoky," Blake said and followed Connor.

Kendall tossed his bag over his shoulder and slid his arms into the straps. He pointed the way as Haley walked beside him.

"What are the actual chances of us getting out of here alive?" She pushed small branches aside and kept walking.

"There are several things that can happen. The wind could shift and turn the blaze away from us, it could rain and help put out the fire, choppers could spot us from the air and send a rescue team in, or we could maintain a positive attitude and keep the pace until one of those options happen." Kendall wiped the perspiration from his forehead. "We're not defeated until we give up."

She gave him a half-hearted smile. "You're right. I'm not jumping any motivational hoops right now, but I know you're right. I've developed a huge respect for the wisdom you've shown through all this."

The wind rustled through the trees while twigs

and pine needles crunched underfoot. Birds sang and squirrels chattered their warnings of approaching danger. Kendall looked into the sky.

Things aren't looking too good for us, Lord. We could use some help.

"You know, I'd never wanted to vacation in the mountains. Beaches were my go-to. It's amazing the number of smells or fragrances that hit your nose all at one time. Like I can smell pine from the pine trees, something musty and something floral. Amazing how we can decipher one from the other even with a blend of smoke." Haley took in another sniff.

Kendall sucked air in through his nose. "You're right, only I'm more prone to smell wood burning and smoke."

"You're trained to detect fire." Haley kicked dried leaves away as she veered a short distance away from him. "It looks more like a path over here. Maybe an animal path."

"I wouldn't get too far away." A cracking sound alerted Kendall of a limb breaking or the threat of a tree falling in the distance. "Sounds like the wind is picking up again."

"The constant whooshing sound would make anyone run for their lives and it's not even as loud as it was earlier," she said.

"Don't let your guard down. That fire can jump and be in front of us in an instant." Kendall eyed the guys ahead of them. They'd grouped together, hiking and talking with an occasional glance behind them. Probably discussing their escape route once they were out of the forest.

"This ground feels strange over here." Haley leaned her body toward him. Her footing was off.

"Haley?" Kendall stepped over and reached for her.

Her foot slipped. She tumbled sideways, then she slid out of sight. Her scream suddenly fell silent.

Chapter Eight

Haley dropped through the smoky air, tumbled against soft, damp soil, then fell through the air again. An abrupt halt in the middle of ferns and vines knocked the wind out of her. Ringing hit her ears.

Ouch!

She lay on the ground, breathless. What happened? Her insides hurt something awful. Spasms attacked her diaphragm. She tried catching a breath. It wouldn't come. Slowly, her breaths came out in tiny huffs. Tears rolled from the pain of trying to breathe.

Why hadn't she rescheduled her vacation? Why was she so worried about losing her deposit? What did it even matter now? She didn't want to die.

She lay still, afraid to move, and tried to calm increasing anxiety. Had she broken a bone or punctured a lung? Tall, swaying trees looked down on her while gray-black smoke boiled upward. Would the tree branches rip away and fall, killing her or hiding her from Kendall, or would that massive cloud of smoke come down and take away what breath she had left? Where was she and where were the others?

The pain in her diaphragm eased. She focused and took in a slow, steady breath, then rolled to her side and sat up. Another breath, easier than before. Her wrist ached a little but didn't seem broken. Everywhere she looked, there was tall foliage masking the layout of the small oblong-shaped ravine or hole or whatever she'd fallen into. There appeared to be no way out.

Only the distant sound of a roaring fire met with her ears. No one called her name. Had they missed her or seen her slip away? Solitude in the middle of nowhere sent panic through her. Should she scream? Would it hurt her diaphragm after falling?

Fear of wild animals wasn't even close to the horror of being stranded down in this gully-type trap. She didn't want to burn alive or be left there alone. Haley pushed to her feet and took in a deep breath. Only a slight tightness remained.

"H-e-l-p. Kendall!" she yelled. "I'm down here."

Could anyone hear her? She fought the panic that still tried to overtake her.

Remain calm. Breathe. Lord, please help me.

A thump and rustling in the foliage made her spin and face the lurking danger. Her pulse increased as goose bumps raced up her arms. She couldn't see what was headed her way in the overgrown weeds, so she stiffened and prepared for a fight.

More movement close to her. Kendall shot up from the tall greenery with a rope tied around his waist. A scream slipped from her lips at his sudden appearance. Haley rushed over and wrapped him in a tight hug.

"Thought I was lost forever." She squeezed tighter. "Thank you for coming for me. Thank you, thank you."

He reciprocated the hug. "Are you hurt?"

"The fall knocked the wind out of me. Thought I'd never breathe again, and my wrist aches a little, but you came for me. I'm so thankful you didn't leave me here."

God, thank You for sending help.

Kendall slowly pushed her arms away. "Did you really think I'd leave you here? I told you to trust me."

"You're right. I knew you'd do what you could to rescue me, but I didn't know how far I'd fallen or if I was out of reach or if you knew I fell."

"Of course I did. I saw you falling, but I couldn't catch you before you slipped out of reach." Kendall untied the rope from his waist and tied it around Haley's. "Blake and his friends are going to pull you up. When I tug on the rope, they'll start pulling. Are you ready?"

"I'm ready." She tightened her grip on the rope as he gave the rope a couple of pulls.

"Here you go. Hold on to the rope. Once you're up, they'll lower it back down for me."

She held on and her feet lifted off the ground. Kendall stood below her, watching over her rescue. She took in a couple of breaths and blew them out.

It was a miracle she hadn't broken any bones. Her scrambled thoughts repeated, *Kendall came for me*.

Thick vines and tall plants blocked her view as she eased upward. Blake and his friends never looked so good standing above the foliage while they tugged on the rope. A glance down showed Kendall still watching and still waiting. Her feet touched the side of the ravine and finally found level ground.

Blake pulled her away from the drop-off and wrapped her in a hug as he untied the rope. "Were you that desperate to get away from us?" A grin smoothed across his face. The look in his eyes told her he cared. Maybe it was a slipup, but that was the Blake she remembered as a child.

"It wasn't on purpose, believe me." She backed up and stood by a tree, thankful they'd rescued her and waiting for them to pull Kendall up.

"If ya keep slowing us down, we'll never outrun this fire." Mac wound the rope up, tossed it over his shoulder and walked away.

"We're wasting time." J.R. kicked the ground. He turned and followed Mac.

"Wait. What are you doing?" Haley ran toward Mac. "We've got to get Kendall."

"We know our way out of here." Connor smirked. "He's taking us in circles to give the cops time to close in."

Her heart pounded relentlessly against her chest. "You can't leave him down there." She grabbed at the rope. Mac pushed her away. "Blake?" Would he side with her?

Blake grabbed Mac by the arm. "Hey, man, we're not leaving him."

"You may have planned the escape, but you're not the boss of me." Mac jerked his arm away. "I agree with Connor. Fire boy has been misleading us. We don't need him anymore."

J.R. stood off to the side with his arms crossed.

Blake jerked at the rope. Mac swung around and punched Blake.

Blake tackled Mac. They rolled on the ground. Connor picked up the Pulaski and lifted it in the air over Blake's head. Haley ran and jumped onto Connor's back. He turned, grabbing at her. She banged her fist against his head. He backed up and bumped her against a tree. She fell to the ground.

Mac and Blake hopped to their feet. Mac tossed the rope on the ground. "Have it your way, but I'm not helping." He backed up and walked away.

"Count me out, too." Connor joined Mac.

Haley propped her hands on her hips. "I cannot believe you guys would—"

Blake's hand touched her shoulder. "Don't waste your breath. You can't reason with some people. Come on." He held the rope up.

Haley rushed to the edge of the ravine. She looked back at Blake, who tied one end of the rope around a tree trunk, then tossed the other end down to Kendall. At the tug of the rope, the two of them pulled Kendall up.

She was safe and Kendall was back on solid ground. Funny how Blake fought with his so-called friends and helped rescue Kendall. Was the hard-core wall around his heart softening?

Her eyes met with Kendall's concerned stare. "Are you okay?"

He chuckled. "I'm fine. You're the one who fell. What took so long?"

Blake rolled the rope up and handed it to Kendall, who put it in his bag. Haley pondered what had just happened. "Mac and Connor had a meltdown. They weren't in favor of pulling you out. Said they knew the way out."

Kendall turned his head toward Mac and Connor, walking in the distance. "I see."

"Blake and I pulled you up while J.R. watched."

Kendall stuck his good hand out and shook Blake's hand. "Thanks, man."

Popping, snapping and hissing filled her ears as the roar grew deafening. They'd been delayed too long and allowed the wildfire time to get too close.

"Come on." Kendall took her hand and pulled her with him.

A pain shot through her wrist. She jerked her hand away and rubbed it.

Kendall's eyebrows lowered.

"It's my wrist." She switched sides and offered her other hand.

"Oh." His long legs walked almost faster than she could run. She forced herself to stay focused and keep up with him. No complaining. She longed for another drink of water.

Blake and J.R. stayed on their heels. They bypassed Mac and Connor, who saw them running and picked up the pace behind them. She guessed they'd decided it was best to stay with the group now that they were in danger again.

Bushes and low-lying limbs slapped her in the face as they ran. Some of them smacked her pretty hard, and she was certain they'd leave welts. Her hair tossed and blew wildly with the unstable wind conditions. Hair covered her eyes, and she wiped it away from her face. If only she had her scrunchie to tie her hair back.

After the fall, all the additional scrapes on her arms and legs seemed trivial. She'd have to watch her wrist, and as long as Kendall's sandals held up, she'd make it. The thought of running barefooted through the woods sent a shudder down her spine. She couldn't think about all the rocks and thorns her feet would encounter.

"Any idea where we're going?" Her voice hitched with every bounce of her feet.

"To the top where the boulders are. We can see for miles up there." He didn't sound as winded as her. He kept a steady gait.

Uphill? Her legs were already exhausted and achy. She must push the dread from her mind and keep going. They'd been slowly rising, but from the looks of the boulders, the climb would grow steeper. Her thighs rebelled. She ignored the threat of cramping crawling up her legs. Her ears popped with the altitude. Or was the fire causing a popping sound in the burning trees?

A spider web hit her face. She let out a squeal, tugged her hand from Kendall's and slapped at her face several times. "Ran into a spider web. Yuck!" She turned her back to Kendall, who had come to an abrupt halt. "Is there anything on my back? Do you see a spider?"

Kendall brushed her back and turned her around. His eyes pierced hers. "You're clear. There's nothing but dirt and grime decorating your clothes." His warm smile helped relax her.

Connor raked his hands over his face, shook his head and spat. "I found one, too."

"I hate spiders. They give me the creeps." She shivered, then took Kendall's hand again.

"I can handle a lot of insects, but spiders are not one of them." Connor wiped his hands on his pants. "They're too small to shoot."

Haley fell in line with Kendall's fast pace and fought to keep going against her body's rebellion.

"After all you've been through the past three days, are you telling me a spider will stop you in your tracks? You are too funny." Kendall shot her a glance. He kept his focus on where they were going.

"Yep. I'm a wimp when it comes to creepy spiders."

J.R. yelled at them to wait, slowed his pace, then stopped. He leaned over with his hands on his knees and took in some deep breaths. Kendall and Haley slowed a minute and waited for J.R, before resuming their fast pace.

"Hey, don't go off and leave us," Connor said.

"Gotta catch my breath." J.R. straightened and blew out a huff before he jogged toward them.

"We're waiting, but I thought you knew the way." Blake put his hands at his waist.

"Don't get smart with me." Connor patted the gun in his waistband.

"Is that a threat?" Blake bowed up.

"Stop. One thing is for sure." Haley took in a deep breath. "This vacation has forced me to pray more than ever. The Bible says to pray continually. Well, now I know what those prayers entail. I've been praying from the moment my eyes popped open back in the cabin when Blake tied me up."

Kendall turned and stumbled into a tree, catching himself before he butted his head. "Must have caught my foot on that protruding tree root." He pushed away. "Let's get going."

"We don't need you getting hurt. You and God are the two getting us out of here. God's leading you and you're leading us. I think that's how it's supposed to work." She let out a moan. Her body was on the verge of collapse. "I don't know how much longer my legs will let me keep torturing them."

Kendall slowed his pace, which loosened his grip on her hand and allowed her to walk rather than run. The other guys caught up and fell in behind them.

Haley counted her blessings that they hadn't been attacked by wild animals. If she didn't see any more for the rest of their journey, she'd be happy. However, squirrels, rabbits and deer were acceptable.

It suddenly dawned on her that there were all

kinds of snakes, bugs and scorpions. Guess adrenaline took over, and she'd totally forgotten about the threats under her feet.

No sooner had those thoughts scrolled through her mind, than Kendall threw his arm out and came to a halt. He pointed to a black bear standing on his hind legs clawing a tree. The bear stopped and turned his head toward them, then hopped down on all fours and faced them.

Haley clutched onto Kendall's shirt. "What are we going to do?"

"Don't anybody make any sudden moves." Kendall reached inside the side pocket of his pack and pulled out his bear spray. "If you run, he will assume the chase is on."

"Got my pistol." Connor's voice was barely above a whisper.

"Me, too." Mac stood beside Haley, holding his weapon ready to shoot.

"You know I've got mine," J.R. chimed in.

"Don't anyone get trigger-happy. He will probably move on if he doesn't consider us a threat." Kendall stood straight with his head up to keep from appearing vulnerable to the bear.

Blake eased up behind Haley. "I've got this Pulaski. If he gets too close and y'all don't kill him first, I'll slam him with the pointed end of this thing."

The bear took a few steps forward, licked his paws, then veered off in the opposite direction. He paused, looked back, then moseyed on into the wilderness. Everyone let go of the breath they'd held.

"They don't normally attack unless they feel threatened. Keep your eyes open, though. He could circle around and come up behind us." Kendall shifted their direction a little more to the right. He'd do what he could to avoid the extra threat. A slight turn in their hiking was the best option anyway.

"The fire has all the wildlife searching for safe ground, just like us. That's why we saw a bear again. Other animals are moving around, too. We just haven't seen them. Normally, they stay out of sight."

The boulders came into view. Still a distance away. His goal was to seek refuge there and rest their legs for a while. The constant stopping wasn't helping, but Kendall was the only one with mountain climbing stamina. They needed whatever time he allowed to get refreshed.

Once again, the boulders weren't the best shelter but would have to do unless they ran across another cave. What was the likelihood of finding another one? If he had his choice, they'd run into another river before dark and make camp next to it. Then, if the fire caught up with them, they could jump in the river.

"I'll keep my eyes open, but you could've left off that last part." Connor put his pistol in his waistband. He looked behind him and off to the sides.

The others did likewise. Kendall pocketed his bear spray and continued his journey.

A gust of hot air rushed by them. Kendall's automatic reaction was to duck and turn, evaluate and act. Swirls of smoke danced behind them. The firestorm had rejuvenated itself. Disappointment and frustration rushed over him. The fire could have flared up from killer trees. Those were the worst. They burned on the inside, then burst into flames and caught everyone off guard or the broken limbs fell against trees and threatened to give way.

"The atmospheric pressure isn't in our favor today and this wind will push the fire forward." Kendall's pace picked up again. "We should be praying for rain."

He didn't hold Haley's hand. Her hiking confidence had increased and apparently her energy level had, too, since she'd remained close behind him. They paved their way through the entangling vines, fallen branches, jagged stones and uneven ground. If she needed his help, she'd offer her hand unless he saw a reason to help her again. Not that he minded. Her small, warm hand fit into his hand perfectly. In fact, she fit into his arms perfectly, too.

Increased heat nipped at their backs. Just how well would the boulders shield them from the rush of scorching heat and the blaze? Would it heat the stone and fry them? Doubts of their safety crept into his thoughts. Would they have time to climb the mountain of boulders before the raging inferno reached them? Not hardly.

Lord, what's the answer here?

"Where are we going?" Blake asked, jogging up beside Kendall. "This heat is intensifying."

"I'm headed toward the boulders, but I'm praying it will shield us as the fire passes." Kendall kept going. No time to stop and ponder directions.

"What do you mean until the fire passes? We can't live through that oven," Mac said.

A cool mist hit Kendall's face while the heat pressed against his back. Mac was right. They wouldn't make it hiding around the boulders. A surge of adrenaline shot through his body. The only reason there would be a cool mist would be from a waterfall. The question was, how steep was the drop-off to the water and how far away?

"I feel a cold mist." Haley tapped Kendall's shoulder.

"I do, too. Could be a waterfall. We're going that direction." Kendall bit his lip.

Please let the waterfall be Your answer. Please.

If his body was giving way to the intensity of the heat, he couldn't imagine how the rest of them were holding up. Burning alive wasn't an option. He started running. In his peripheral vision, he noted Haley had some newfound strength and was right on his heels, as were the three escapees and the security guard. They ran downhill and burst through the trees at the shore of a huge waterfall flowing from somewhere under the boulders above where they'd originally headed. The foliage stopped at the edge of the small river.

"Look. Follow me." Kendall sloshed water as he ran along the narrow riverbank and curved behind the waterfall. A damp, cave-like indentation in the rock formation behind the waterfall was wider than it originally looked.

He spun and helped Haley over the wet rocks and stayed there to assist the men in case any of them slipped. Not that they'd admit to needing help, but at least he was willing.

"Thank You, Lord." Haley held her hands in the air and danced in place, then glanced at the other guys. "Thank You, thank You, thank You." She blew out a relieved sigh.

Kendall joined the escapees as they watched her with their eyebrows lowered and questioning looks on their faces. He guessed she was doing her happy dance. He'd join her if he didn't think the guys would harass him.

"What's wrong with you?" Connor shook his head at Haley.

She lowered her arms and walked up to him. "We aren't safe because we found a waterfall. We're safe because God is taking care of us and directing our steps. It's called trust. And I'm trusting He will get us all out of here safely."

Kendall recalled the prayers he'd prayed since they had been on the run. "So, do you think God sent the bear to deter us from the direction we were going to the boulders?"

Haley paused and pursed her lips. Lips he wanted to kiss. He pushed the thoughts aside. Building a relationship wasn't in his job description. At least, not right now.

She tapped her foot on the wet rock. "We will

never know why things happen the way they do, but I believe God can do anything. I don't know if God used the bear, but I'd like to think He did because that's when we changed directions. Regardless, we are away from the blaze."

Something crashed into the river. Kendall spun and walked to the edge along the side of the waterfall. A tree half ablaze and half smoldering. The foliage by the water burned. He jumped back when another tree fell almost on top of the waterfall. The mist from the water kept them cool. They'd escaped the inferno by mere seconds.

"Might as well get comfortable. These trees will burn awhile." Kendall tossed his pack to the back of the cave, where a tiny stream of water rolled toward the river. He found a dry spot and pointed it out to Haley.

"Thanks. My legs are ready for a break." She sat and leaned against the wall. "Why are these walls slick? The other cave had rough and jagged walls. Does it flood in here?"

"I imagine at some point the water smoothed out the stone, but I'm not a cave and waterfall expert, so what do I know?" Kendall sat within an arm's length from Haley.

"Thought you knew everything, fire boy." J.R. tossed a small rock toward the waterfall.

"Not so much. I've been through handcrew training and I'm still studying for more promotions. Rescuing Haley and running into you guys has put me through a multitude of hands-on experiences. We've been running from a fire that nipped at our heels and seemed to have us in its crosshairs." Kendall took off his hard hat and scratched his head. "Never expected to be in this position."

"What caused you to help these guys escape, Mr. J.R., prison guard? Why betray a reputable job only to run for your own freedom?" Haley's question turned their heads.

Kendall wanted to know too but hadn't found the right moment to ask.

J.R. sneered at Haley, but his expression softened. He picked up several small stones and tossed them sideways to the water before he spoke.

"Life had grown mundane. It was the same old, same old every day. Go home late, get up early, listen to all the bickering by hundreds of men who all claimed innocence, knowing full well they were guilty." He tossed another rock and looked at his comrades. "These guys started talking to me, acting like they gave a rip. When they asked if I'd like to add some adventure to my life, I was all ears. I had to think about it a while before making a decision."

"Yep." Mac stretched his legs out and rested his head against the stone wall.

"And he finally agreed and gave us tips on what to do and the best time to take action. He left us weapons by the dumpster and said he'd meet up with us at a designated place with some civilian clothes. Now you know everything."

"But don't you have families? What good will it do if you're caught and have to spend even more time in prison? Doesn't that defeat your purpose?" Haley's widened eyes stayed fixed on the escapees.

"My wife died last year in a car wreck and I don't have a family. I have nothing to go home to, so why not add a little excitement to my life?" J.R. rubbed his nose and looked away. Was that regret that shot across his face?

Kendall couldn't imagine giving up his freedom to help convicts escape. They'd committed crimes and needed to pay their dues. How could escaping prison make things any better for them? Making responsible decisions wasn't in their plans, only getting away and surviving. Would Haley's probing into their personal lives rekindle anger and be the determining factor in whether they let her and him go or kill them?

Chapter Nine

"What about you, Connor?" Haley refused to back down. These guys had families that their irresponsible decisions would affect.

"Why are you poking your nose in other folks' lives?" Connor narrowed his brows and eyed her. "It ain't none of your business."

"True, but all of you have someone who loves you, and what you're doing only hurts them more." Haley pulled her legs up to her chest and wrapped her arms around them.

"Escaping sounded intriguing and I like tough challenges." Mac spoke up. "Figured I'd get to see my wife and two kids sooner. We would move away and have a new life in Hawaii after I robbed a few banks and got us a couple of bags of cash. Didn't think about getting caught and what that meant for them."

"My brother said he'd meet me in California. He's rented a condo close to the beach," Connor said.

"We'll live off our parents' inheritance and hang out on the beach for the rest of our lives. I'm gonna change my identity so no one can find me."

Haley turned to her cousin. "Blake, what about you?"

Blake raked his hand across the cave floor and brushed up a small pile of sand and pebbles. He pursed his lips and looked up at her. "Still debating on what my next move will be. Me and the guys had everything planned out, but after trying to escape this prison of fire, I'd be better off hanging out in my cell."

"Aw, man, you don't mean that," Mac said. "What's gotten into you?"

"Thinking about my parents and how disappointed they are in me, well, especially my mom, kinda twists an ache in my gut. Dad likes to watch the world through the bottom of a whiskey bottle, so his sense of time is diluted and hazy."

"Stop talking nonsense, Blake." Connor sat up and turned to Haley. "We celebrated all the way to your cabin once he saw your name on the registry. When J.R. arrived, we stashed those jumpsuits in your car." Then he yawned and scooted down against the wall. "Thanks for leaving it unlocked."

"Unbelievable." Haley twisted a strand of hair and pulled out a leaf.

"Some guy showed up at your cabin door demanding your satellite phone. We had to take him down so he couldn't identify us. Then Kendall and those other firefighters came barreling inside. We scuffled a minute and ran out the door." Mac chewed on a piece of grass. "Falling backward and knocking yourself out wasn't part of the plan. We did what we had to do. Couldn't carry you, so we ran."

"He's not dead," Kendall said. "One of my team members helped him to safety."

Connor sat up. "You mean he got away and now the police know about us?"

"Where have you been, Connor?" Blake tossed a small stone at Connor. "I can just hear the top story on the morning news, 'Forest Service firefighter rescues female from cabin and is taken hostage by three escapees and a rogue prison guard. These men are considered armed and dangerous. Blah, blah, blah.'"

The four men chuckled, but Haley didn't see the humor in any of it. Kendall wasn't amused, either. She caught him looking at her with a disgusted look on his face. She couldn't agree more. If she'd learned anything about trust from her ex-boyfriend and her cousin, she'd learned it didn't come easy. Trust was something you earned.

Good thing she didn't have to earn God's salvation, or she would have failed a long time ago. Even now, her annoyance with Blake and his friends gnawed at her. She needed to keep asking forgiveness because she still had a negative attitude toward them. But she'd keep those thoughts to herself.

A scorpion skittered across the cave floor. Haley jumped to her feet at the same time Kendall did. She let out a squeal, but quickly covered her mouth. The men didn't need anything else to nag her about. Mac drew his legs up and they all watched until Kendall pushed it into the water with his foot.

A shudder rushed over Haley's body. The creature appeared out of nowhere. "Those things are poisonous, aren't they?"

"Most scorpions' stings are more like a bee sting. They can kill insects, but to people, they are painful and sometimes cause nausea." Kendall walked to the edge of the waterfall. "A few of them are dangerous, so it's best not to mess with them. I've heard that the death stalker scorpion is the worst, but it's in Africa."

"Death stalker or night crawler, you don't have to worry about me messing with any of them." Were there more where that one came from? Her eyes squinted as she checked along the edges of the cave, the walls and the ceiling.

She stood and stretched before joining Kendall at the opening of the cave. The spray of the waterfall cooled her sweaty skin. Heat from the flaming trees and underbrush on the other side of the waterfall seeped into the cave. An occasional cloud of smoke filtered in, but quickly dissipated.

Her foot slipped on the wet rock. Kendall caught her around the waist before she hit the floor. He pulled her close and kept his muscular arm around her. The warmth of his touch comforted her and made her feel safe. If only she could stay by his side.

"How long will we have to stay here?" She cut her eyes up at him. His gaze bore into hers. Right there in front of all those escapees, she wanted him to kiss her. Could he see the welcome in her eyes?

Was she reading his expression correctly, or was he merely concerned about getting her home?

"Depends on the behavior of the fire and weather. Wind, as you've learned through this nightmare, is a controlling force." He kept eye contact and paused.

Would he please quit taunting her like that? Could he feel her trying to steady her breathing? The guys' voices echoed behind them as they talked about prison stuff, in which she had no interest. Their voices faded as her focus remained on Kendall.

He broke eye contact. Disappointment loomed over the lost romantic moment with him. She closed her eyes and turned her head. His free hand touched her cheek and his lips brushed across hers. Her toes curled in his sandals, and in an instant, his lips were gone.

"Once the intensity of the storm passes, we may walk in the stream as long as it doesn't get too deep." Kendall spoke as though nothing had happened between them. "The flow of the water may lead us to fresh soil where we would be more likely to meet up with a rescue team."

She stepped away and allowed his arm to drop from around her waist. Maybe it was the predicament they were in that made her more vulnerable. Maybe he saw her longing for a kiss, and he acted on it, or maybe he wanted to kiss her like she did him. He hadn't showed either way.

Haley brushed at her clothes to take her mind off his brief kiss. Dirt and grime smeared even worse. If her clothes looked that disgusting, she could only imagine how her face and hair looked, and yet, he'd kissed her, however slight it might have been. She'd never forget that moment.

"What's wrong?"

He would ask.

"Nothing really. I'm looking forward to getting home. I'm worried about my parents and how all this has affected my dad's heart condition. Maybe someday you'll get to see me without all this dirt and grime, that is, if our paths cross again." She pushed her hair back behind her ears and turned away. She longed for a shower and a hot meal.

His hand clutched her arm, and she looked back at him. "I'm counting on it." The seriousness of his expression didn't change. "I plan to see you when this is all over."

Her heart thrashed against her chest. He wanted to see her again. Anticipation battled against weariness. If Kendall was a dream, she didn't want to wake up.

"I'd like that."

Mac's deep voice echoed. "What's up with the fire now?"

"Still raging." Kendall slid between the waterfall and the cave, then stepped back inside. "It can burn for days, but when the heat intensity dies down, I figure we'll follow the stream out of here."

Connor jumped to his feet. His eyes were wide and his breathing sounded strained. "These walls are closing in on me. I can't just sit around here waiting for the cops to raid the place and handcuff me."

"What are you going to do? Run through the fire?"

Mac said. "Sorry, but I'm not into burned toast. I'm waiting for Kendall's all clear."

"Don't you get it? We're cornered by staying here." Connor paced around the cave like a caged lion. His face whitened.

"You've been breathing too much smoke. Do you hear yourself? You're not being reasonable." Blake stretched out on the floor and put his arms over his eyes. "I'm resting while I can."

Haley's thoughts drifted back again to her mom and dad. His surgery was coming up, and her mom would be beside herself with worry. Haley longed to be there for her, holding her hand and offering encouragement. She glanced around the cave. These men would either go back to prison or find a way to avoid capture, although she couldn't imagine how. Rangers and police would rush the area as soon as it was safe.

Kendall backed away from the cave's opening and sat back down. He dumped his dwindling supply of snacks on the ground. "Here you go! Eat slow and make it last."

Blake rose up and snatched the remaining beef jerky. Mac and J.R. grumbled about granola and protein bars. J.R. slid his backpack behind him.

"What's up with that pack you're carrying?" Mac reached for the small pack.

"None of your business." J.R. pulled it closer.

Mac dived for the backpack and tugged it out of J.R.'s hand. "You've been hanging on to this the whole time. What's so important that you don't want us to see what's inside?"

Connor still paced like a wild animal, ready to bolt.

"If you're not eating yours, Connor, I'll take it," Blake said.

Mac unzipped the bag and dumped the contents. Six small bottled waters rolled across the cave floor and a mixture of snacks spilled out. "Seriously? You've been holding out on us all this time? Some partner you are. How much have you had behind our backs?"

"Not much. I've been saving it for us." J.R. retrieved his backpack but left the contents on the floor.

"Sure you have." Mac grabbed a pack of peanut butter and crackers and a bottle of water and sat back. "I'm keeping an eye on you. What else are you hiding from us?"

"Nothing. This is it." J.R. raked a hand over his unshaven face. "You found it at a good time."

Haley walked over and picked up another granola bar and a bottled water. She rose up, and Connor grabbed her from behind, putting his pistol to her temple. Sweat beaded on his forehead.

"I'm getting out of here." Connor's hot breath brushed past her cheek. "If I take her, maybe you'll get us out of here faster." His glare bore into Kendall.

"Think about what you're doing." Blake stepped forward.

"Like I said, I'm leaving and I'm taking her with me." Connor's grip tightened around her waist.

Kendall's eyes narrowed, and his lips tightened. "You'll have to get past me first."

Haley dropped the bottled water and crackers. Her frightened expression ripped at Kendall's gut. He couldn't let anything happen to her, and he certainly couldn't let Connor leave with her. Neither of them would make it a quarter of a mile with that inferno outside. His fingers dug into his palms as he squeezed his fists. Adrenaline surged through his body. He pondered which defensive tactic would work to free Haley from Connor's grip.

First, he had to get that gun away from her head. A slip of the finger and she'd be gone. He couldn't let Connor keep the upper hand. Kendall liked Haley. He wanted to get to know her better, and he'd tell her so, but in his attempt to escape the fire and get them all to safety, he concluded now was not the time.

Blake reached out his hand. "Put the gun down. You don't want to do that."

"I'm tired of y'all fooling around and dragging me through this forest." He nodded toward Kendall. "We don't know where he's taking us. Probably hoping we will wear down and surrender. Well, that ain't happening. I'm going while I can."

Kendall glanced to see the reaction of the other three. Not that he cared what they thought, but he had to know if they were going to join Connor and face off against him. He'd give his life to protect Haley. Mac and J.R. raised their pistols toward Connor.

"No one's going anywhere," Mac said. He tossed the twig he'd been chewing on the floor. "Calm down and let Haley go. Don't make me shoot you."

"We have to stick together like we agreed until we reach our destination." J.R. lifted his weapon higher. "Now, let her go. We're following our plan."

Connor hid behind Haley and dragged her out of the cave backward. Once they'd cleared the waterfall, Kendall rushed to the opening and peered around the rock wall. Connor turned her with his back to the cave, grabbed the back of her shirt and pushed her forward over the smoldering grass and brush at the edge of the river. An endless thin cloud of smoke hung in the air.

"We won't make it through here, Connor." Haley's voice remained calm. "Maybe we could wait until the fire dies down."

"Quit trying to talk me out of getting away." Connor's voice shook.

Kendall eased out of the cave. He admired Haley's self-control in such a dangerous situation, and her efforts to try talking Connor down. Such a brave lady.

A blazing limb fell and barely missed them. Connor jerked her back from the intense heat, lifted the hand holding the gun and wiped his head with the butt of the weapon. Kendall took advantage of the moment and dived for Connor, pushing Haley away. Out of his peripheral vision, he noted she had stumbled on the uneven ground and fell in the shallow edge of the water.

Kendall landed on top of Connor on the hot riverbank. Good thing it wasn't flaming, or their clothes would've caught on fire. The ground was still warm, but not unbearable. Connor pointed his gun at Kendall. Kendall held his arm in the air and forced the gun away from his face.

J.R. and Mac intervened. They tugged Kendall away about the time a thick cloud of dark gray smoke rolled across the river, sucking the semi-fresh smoky air from the area. Everyone started coughing. Mac grabbed Connor's arm and slammed the hand holding the pistol on a rock. A shot rang out, and Haley screamed and coughed. The weapon dropped to the ground and J.R. scooped it up.

Blake and Kendall ran to Haley, who held on to her arm. Blood soaked the sleeve of her T-shirt. Kendall's pulse thundered. Kendall pushed her sleeve up.

"Just a flesh wound," Blake said. "She'll live."

"She'd better. This shouldn't have happened," Kendall fumed. He helped Haley up and escorted her back inside the cave, with Blake following close behind. "You'll be okay. We'll get it fixed up."

Mac and J.R. walked Connor inside and sat him between them against the opposite wall.

Kendall zeroed his focus in on Connor and pointed at him. "You guys better get control of him. We've got too much to worry about without another outburst."

Connor rubbed his forehead.

"He's okay. Just edgy. Running from the forest fire is enough to take us all over the edge." Mac drew a leg up and rested his arm on top of his knee. "Won't happen again."

"It burns something fierce." Haley tightened her lips.

"I've been shot before." Blake pulled up his shirt and exposed his scar. "Owner of the gas station I tried to rob surprised me with a pistol. Knocked me to the ground. I held my shoulder and screamed. Yours is trivial compared to mine."

Kendall lowered his eyebrows at Blake. "No gunshot wound is trivial. They hurt and there's always the risk of infection. Haley, scream if you want. These grown men would yell and moan if they got shot."

Her tear-filled eyes looked up at him. He hurt for her. He should have protected her better. Who knew Connor was not feeling like himself? He'd keep an eye on him from now on.

"I've got my first aid kit in my bag." Kendall emptied his bag and opened the plastic container. A couple of Band-Aids remained, along with some small alcohol pads and a travel-size antibacterial cream. Not much, but it would have to do.

Blake slowly tore the sleeve of her shirt off. "Don't need all that dirt on an open wound."

Kendall kneeled beside Haley and inspected her arm. "I didn't see this happening." He opened an alcohol pad. "This is going to burn even worse but will subside as it dries. Are you ready?"

"No, but go ahead." She took in a deep breath and held it.

Kendall dabbed at the wound and cleaned around it where the skin had torn away. She turned her head and started blowing on it. "Wow. That smarts."

"Like I said, the burning sensation will level off." So much for trying to console her verbally. He'd rather hold her in his arms and let her know everything was going to be okay.

Blake stood over him, watching and listening to every word. Kendall refrained from any appearance of attraction to Haley to keep from being harassed. Should he care? No. But he did. If these guys knew Kendall cared for Haley, they'd use her as leverage for whatever task came to mind. They already had. Apparently, they hadn't seen him kiss her earlier, or Blake would have reprimanded him and he'd never hear the end. Best to distance himself from her until after the rescue.

He dabbed on the antibacterial cream and put the two Band-Aids over her wound. They weren't big enough to cover the raw flesh completely, but it was better than nothing.

"Will this help?" Blake passed him the piece of her shirtsleeve he'd torn off.

"Thanks." Kendall turned the fabric inside out, looking for the cleanest side, and wrapped around her arm. "It will have to do for now. Paramedics will do a better job once we're rescued."

Kendall studied Haley's face. Her eyes focused on something over his shoulder. He turned and understood her stare. Connor sat back with his head leaned against the cave wall, watching her. Kendall stiffened. He took in a couple of slow breaths and willed himself to relax. Haley's stare remained on Connor. What was she thinking?

"Would you have really killed me?" A frown replaced the hard look she gave him.

Connor wiped a hand over his face. "I don't know. For a moment, the cave walls closed in on me and I had to get away."

"We're going to make it." Haley's voice softened.

Connor slapped at the dirt on his pants leg. "Hope I didn't hurt you too bad."

Kendall left Haley's side, handed her the crackers and bottled water she'd dropped, and returned to his original seat along the opposite wall. He settled in and repacked his bag from where he'd dumped everything out. He sensed Haley looking at him, but he refused to lock eyes. He scolded himself for taking his focus off the main purpose of rescuing all of them and protecting Haley. He'd have to keep reminding himself that now wasn't the time to develop a relationship. The stress of their circumstances could mislead their attraction.

His stomach churned as he struggled with his feelings versus his responsibilities. He'd protect everyone and do his best to get them to safety, but it was the authority's responsibility to apprehend these guys. Kendall figured if he didn't look into Haley's big brown eyes, he wouldn't be captivated by them and sway from the task at hand.

She needed medical attention for that bullet scrape before it got infected and for that knot on her head, not to mention all the scrapes and cuts she'd endured. He needed to get his hand looked at, too, although it had quit hurting. He'd done all he knew to do for their wounds. They'd trained him as an EMT along with firefighting classes, but he wasn't a paramedic.

He knew enough to apply antibiotic cream and cover it with a band-aid. Maybe he should add medical classes to his increasing education list and get his paramedic license as well as his bachelor's degree. Education was always beneficial and could increase his pay.

"That gunshot could have been a fatal blow if the projectile hit any of us in the right place." J.R. hooked his weapon on his belt. "Another outrage like that, and it may not end well for you."

Connor's eyes narrowed. "Are you threatening me?"

"Just stating a fact." J.R. leaned his head back. "I'm gettin' some shut-eye before we make a run for it again."

"It's a good idea if everyone gets some rest." Kendall yawned. "Someone needs to stand watch and make sure we don't get a surprise visit from one of our furry friends."

"I thought we were safe in here and could let our guard down." Haley finger-combed her hair, pulled it up in a ponytail and twisted it into a knot on top of her head. She let out a quiet moan moving her wounded arm.

Her hairdo brought back memories of Kendall's grandmother. She always wore her hair on top of her head. He'd often wondered how she kept it there before he'd discovered she used hairpins. Amazing how people learn to fix long hair without rubber bands or those colorful, stretchy things. He quickly diverted his eyes when she looked up at him.

"Basically, yes, we are safe here, but with the blaze rumbling, one never knows how animals will react. I'd like to think they're running for their lives in the opposite direction." He settled back and leaned on his pack. "I'll take the first hour's watch. Who wants to go next?"

"I can go next." Haley still held her injured arm. "Who can sleep with a throbbing arm and the possibility of another scorpion scrambling through here?"

"I'll take it." Blake nodded at Haley. "You try to get some rest."

She leaned back and munched on her snack.

Who could keep their eyes open between the noise of the firestorm and the constant flow of the waterfall? The sound mimicked about five hundred large mechanic shop fans sitting side by side on high speed. His grandmother's single window fan on the farm lulled him to sleep many times even as an adult, but inside the cave, the magnified rhythm was enough to knock anyone out without medication.

Haley pulled her legs up close to her chest and rested her arms over her knees. She rested her head on her arms, while protecting the sore arm. If he were the man he should be, he'd let her lean on him. He shifted his eyes and checked each person. Amazingly, no one argued about sleep. It was the one thing they all agreed on. Kendall rubbed his face, then his eyes. One slip-up and he'd be snoring, too.

Connor slid to the floor and closed his eyes. Kendall studied him. If he was right, everyone had the same feeling about finding the end of their mountain escape. He wanted to go home as much as the rest of them, and the forest was his job. He still loved firefighting, but being chased by the flames without his team didn't sit well.

J.R.'s eyes were closed. His hand rested on his weapon as though someone might steal it. Kendall still couldn't imagine betraying his teammates like J.R. betrayed his coworkers. What kind of person would throw their life away like that? Desperate ones, he guessed, or possibly someone so lonely that the challenge of pulling off an escape gave them a disillusioned sense of accomplishment.

Mac and Blake were already snoring. Haley shifted her head a few times, trying to get comfortable. Kendall leaned his head against the wall and monitored the waterfall. Flames danced like a light show through the falling water just outside the cave.

Lord, if You sent us here to keep us safe, thank You. Haley says You want us to forgive one another like You forgave us. Well, I know it's no secret that my dad and I haven't had much to do with each other in a while. I'd really like to be in good graces with him. I love him. I'd like to get this promotion, but mostly, I'd appreciate it if You'd show us the way out of here. Thanks.

Blake rose up as though he had an alarm clock.

He pointed to Kendall without saying a word. Kendall nodded and stared at the waterfall. Rescue must come soon. With only a small bottle of water for each of them and minimal snacks, thanks to J.R.'s secret stash, they'd run out of energy to keep going, making all their efforts running from the blaze futile.

Chapter Ten

Haley's arm burned and throbbed. She dozed a few times, but it wasn't home. She longed for her pillow-top mattress and her soft pillow. Her heart ached for her parents. Being an only child born in their later years, she put a lot of responsibility on herself to make sure they had everything they needed. It only made sense that she would be by her mom's side when they wheeled her dad away for heart surgery.

Her job loss suddenly carried no weight. She'd find another dental assistant job and might even move out of the city. Despite the horror of her circumstances, she discovered she loved nature and the quiet serenity of the forest. Not that she wanted to live in a cabin in the woods. Not in the least. An apartment or a home close by might not be a bad idea. She could handle enjoying her coffee every morning with the beauty of the mountains within view. Just the thought held a peaceful image.

Then there was Kendall. She turned her head to

where she could look at him. He sat with his hands behind his head and leaned against the wall, staring at the waterfall. Or that's what it looked like. His eyes closed and in a moment's time, his breathing deepened. Didn't look like he had a problem going to sleep. She guessed it was because of his forest job, and he was used to sleeping most anywhere.

His broad chest rose and fell with each heavy breath. She'd grown to like him more than she'd expected. Her hand fit in his perfectly and she connected with him like a lost puzzle piece put back in place. He'd acted like he cared for her more than just an acquaintance needing rescuing or, as he'd put it, a damsel in distress. His warm breath on her face when he leaned and brushed his lips against hers was like the flutter of butterfly wings before it flew away. It imprinted the moment in her memory. Never had she had such a feeling of belonging.

Blake punched Mac. His voice was barely audible above the noisy waterfall. "Your turn to watch."

Mac grunted. He pushed to his feet and walked to the mouth of the cave. He reached his hand out and let the water splash on it, then rubbed his face.

Haley got the idea she could wet her hair and get some of the grime out when it was her turn to keep watch. She'd wash her face, too. Maybe that would rejuvenate her somewhat.

Her gaze reverted to Kendall. He'd suddenly become distant after the bullet grazed her. Had her assumptions of a relationship or connection between them been wrong? If so, why the kiss? Had he gotten caught up in the moment, or was it her fault? Guess after their rescue she'd find the answer. She had to get a grip and quit thinking about getting to know him. Surviving weighed higher.

Mac walked over to Connor, but Haley shook her head and volunteered to stand watch. He resumed his position on the floor and went right to sleep. His immediate snores proved it. She pushed to her feet and approached the waterfall and found a steady stream of water, not as powerful as the rest. She splashed water on her face first, then bent over, stuck her head under the water and scrubbed like she had shampoo.

Ah, it felt good. She stepped back, squeezed the water from her hair, and slung her head back. Her breath caught. Kendall stood beside her. His questioning eyes searched her.

"You scared me." She spoke softly in hopes of not waking the other guys. Why was he looking at her like she had four heads?

"Didn't mean to frighten you. How's your arm?" He backed up and put a space between them. Why? Had she done something wrong?

"It throbs and stings, but I'm okay. Could've been worse." She turned and finger-combed her hair as best as she could with all the tangles. At least most of the grass and leaves were gone.

"How's your hand?"

"Doesn't hurt anymore."

When she tossed her head back, Kendall still watched her. She couldn't read his eyes to get a clue of what he was thinking.

"You want some more of the medicine on your arm?"

"Not yet. Let's save it in case I need it later." She backed up to the wall opposite him and leaned against it. "How much longer do we need to wait here?"

"After everyone wakes up, I'll step out and test the perimeters and behavior of the fire. The wind is a big factor, too. If the heat is bearable, we'll leave, but for now, this is the safest place for us." Kendall shifted his eyes to the waterfall.

Why wouldn't he look at her when he talked?

"Have I offended you?" Haley studied his solemn expression. "If so, I didn't mean to."

He glanced at her, but quickly diverted his eyes. "No, not at all. It's just, well, in our best interest to keep our focus on getting out of here. If things work out later, maybe we can meet up for dinner or something."

"So, what you're saying is I am a distraction. Is that it?"

"Sort of. I've got a job to do and letting you get to me distracts my focus and reasoning." He kicked a small stone into the water.

Haley wasn't sure if he meant that as a good thing or bad. Did he not want to hold her hand anymore and steady her as they run from the fire? He'd saved her life four times already. Had he grown weary of saving her and now he found her too needy? Her thoughts reeled. Was she making a big deal out of nothing? Her eyes filled with tears. What was going on with her emotions?

She reached her hand out to the water and splashed some on her face. The last thing she wanted him to see was the disappointment or the confusion over what he'd said. She hadn't asked him to help her. He was the one who rescued her from the burning cabin.

"I see." She steadied her voice. "I'll do my best to stay out of your way." She turned and walked deeper into the cave. When she turned around, Kendall still watched her. His solemn expression was unreadable. She dropped her eyes and decided she'd comply with his wishes. She'd put distance between them. Maybe Blake would help her if she needed it.

Connor stirred and opened his eyes. He sat up. "My turn."

Kendall returned to where he'd sat previously, across from her. He never looked in her direction. Not so much as a glance. How could she have been so wrong in her evaluation of him? How foolish had she been being so goo-goo eyed over him? She touched her face, noting how warm her cheeks were. Embarrassment revealed itself. The hurt of rejection, once again, stung deep.

Haley closed her eyes to keep from looking at Kendall. Frustration coiled itself around her confused thoughts. She could only be upset with herself, but he played a role in making her think he cared for her. Ugh. How could she have fallen for him so quickly?

I'll be myself, keep my distance, and not get in

Kendall's way. Time will tell if we are meant to be together. Lord, help me.

Loud cracking and a sudden pop shot everyone to their feet. In a moment's time, the top of a burning tree fell into the waterfall and partially into the cave. Heat and boiling smoke filled the cave, while flames consumed the top of the tree.

Haley tugged the bandanna over her mouth and nose. Her eyes watered from the smoke.

"We've got to get out of here before we suffocate." Kendall tossed his pack over onto his back. "Follow me and be careful. The branches and tree trunk are still hot."

He climbed over the smoldering part of the tree where the waterfall had put out the flames. Water splashed and stirred more smoke. Haley tightened the straps of his sandals across the top of her foot. Blake's hand landed on her back.

"Go, Haley, I've got your back." Blake's attitude had changed, and he showed genuine concern for her safety. She'd have to ask him later what happened.

She stretched her leg over a long branch. The heat grew stronger, and the smoke made it difficult to see exactly where she stepped. A hand, Kendall's hand, stretched through the waterfall. She took his hand, and his strength pulled her through so fast she landed in his arms. His intense eyes pierced her watering eyes, confusing her emotions.

Kendall fought the powerful urge to pull her close and hold her. She'd made it past the danger unscathed. Instead, he steadied her on her feet, and they stepped back while the others made their way into the open air.

Everyone coughed and rubbed their eyes. More sizzling, popping and cracking alerted Kendall to the urgency of their situation. They had to hurry. He did not know which way these trees would fall. Some stood tall and burned all the way up. Not every tree would tumble to the ground, but he couldn't take any chances. Now was the time to follow the stream and pray for safety from flying embers. The heat was extreme but bearable, especially since they had the water to help cool their skin.

"Where do we go now?" Connor wiped his face with his shirttail. Fear shone in his eyes.

"Straight ahead in this stream. We'll have an obstacle course with all the debris, but it's our only option." Kendall waved his arm. "This way."

The knee-deep water quickly rose until it reached their waists. His boots squished in the rocky, muddy earth beneath his feet. He could only imagine the trouble Haley experienced with his sandals on. Kendall pressed forward, thankful he'd paid attention in class and studied about forest fires and their behaviors. Although, this situation wasn't part of the training. He had to use common sense and pray for wisdom and guidance.

"I feel every rock under my feet." Haley waded into the water behind him. "But I'm thankful I at least have something to keep them from cutting me."

"This wasn't the way I wanted to wake up," Mac

hollered above the diminishing roar. "Why is it getting quieter? Is it the calm before the storm, so to speak?"

"Could be the change in weather, the direction of the wind or any number of things." Kendall stopped. A small, charred tree blocked their path. "Come help me move this out of the way. Haley, you stand back."

All five men heaved, lifted the tree and tossed it on the bank, then they all proceeded through the stream. The scent of wood burning had always been a pleasant memory for Kendall. His grandparents had a wood-burning stove they used to heat their small farmhouse. They'd even let him toss a short log or two into the stove and poke the coals until the blaze returned. He enjoyed those memories, but forest fires took on a whole new meaning and created a lot more danger.

"There's a slight current about ankle deep. Does anyone feel it?" Haley asked.

"It's not bad," Blake said. "I'd rather have the undertow than be walking over all that burned ground. At least this water keeps us cool."

"My thoughts exactly." Mac's deep voice was unmistakable. "I'd stop and swim a while if things were different."

"I can't swim." Connor's voice sounded a little shaky. "As long as it doesn't get any deeper, I'll be okay."

Kendall kept his eyes peeled on the surrounding conditions. He noted the stream wasn't so much a stream anymore. It slowly widened, which could be good or bad. They would be fine as long as the undertow didn't grow stronger and develop rapids. It could lead them to another waterfall, which wouldn't be in their best interest, or it could push them downstream where the water might join a river. If he read the map correctly, he'd guess it was another waterfall, only much larger.

Haley remained quiet. He'd like to know what she was thinking. Apparently, he'd hurt her feelings, which wasn't his intention. He shouldn't have said anything earlier. He really liked her, and now there was tension between them. Something he hoped to straighten out when they reached the command center.

J.R. yelled from the rear. His voice fell flat in the forest. "My gun's getting wet. I'm going to walk on the riverbank."

"Go ahead." Kendall turned and looked back. The underbrush and grass along the edge of the water still burned and smoldered. "The ground may be too hot. Might be okay if you have on boots, but tennis shoes and Haley's sandals won't survive."

"You mean your melted sandals won't survive? Not that I'm complaining. I'm thankful for them." She held her arms above the water.

The bandage on her wounded arm had turned red. Blood soaked through the Band-Aids and dripped into the water. Even though it was mountain water, that didn't mean it was sterile. There were all kinds of bacteria in that stream.

An odd but familiar noise hit Kendall's ears. He

spun just as a blaze burst out from the inside of a tree and shot fire embers into the sky. "Look out."

Mac jumped into the water, and high-stepped it to catch up with them. "What was that?"

"It's what we call hazard trees. They burn from the inside out. Broken limbs that catch on other limbs up in the trees are called snags. These have the potential of falling and hurting someone." Kendall threw his hand up and stopped everyone.

"What is it?" Haley stepped up beside him, but not too close, he noticed.

He pointed at another smoldering tree blocking their river path. In the not-too-far distance, the water merged into a larger body of water and developed rapids. Without a boat or raft, it wasn't safe for them to ride it out. They had no other option but to continue their journey on the charred ground once they reached that tree.

"We've got to get out of the water. It's too dangerous ahead." Kendall faced the group and pointed to the threat.

"Can't we build a raft?" Mac's eyebrows lifted.

"What do you plan to use as building material? Look around." Kendall couldn't believe Mac even suggested building a raft. Everything within sight was burning, burned or smoldering.

"Guess you're right." Mac turned slightly toward the shoreline. "Wasn't thinking."

Kendall noted the closer they got to the tree that blocked their passage, the stronger the undertow became. Broken tree limbs and debris floated toward them. Something hit his leg underwater and knocked him off his feet. His body slammed against the fallen tree, but he grabbed hold of a limb. The rushing water against his calves tugged against the strength in his legs and pulled him under.

He heaved his body upright until his feet touched the ground. He gasped for air and let out a groan as he made his way onto dry land. Mac, Blake, J.R. and Connor stood on the shore wringing out their wet clothes.

"Haley." His heart sank. "Where's Haley?" He spun and searched the rapids. Had the water swept her under like him? Was she trapped in the limbs, drowning? Had the undertow swept her downstream?

Kendall jumped back into the water. More splashes followed behind him.

"Form a human chain but be careful. This water will suck you under when you least expect it. Let's see if she's wedged somewhere around the tree." Kendall's voice cracked. He couldn't lose her. Not like this.

"Hurry or she'll drown." Blake dived underwater.

Kendall took in a deep breath and dived underwater. He held on to large, extending limbs and reached around the rushing water with one hand. Panic rose inside him, but he pushed it away as best as he could. He had to focus. An ache stung in his lungs. He needed air. Still moving along the length of the tree, holding on to different branches, he popped out of the water. He took another deep breath and continued searching. His arm touched another arm. He grabbed it and a hand pushed it away. Kendall surfaced again and Blake appeared, then Mac. His heart sank.

"Anything?" Kendall blinked the water from his eyes.

"She's not here." Mac turned and pulled himself toward the shore.

"I can't give up." Kendall's pulse raced.

"Me, either." Blake took another breath and disappeared underwater.

Kendall did likewise. Haley had to be okay. He hand-walked himself underwater, limb by limb, to an area where the current almost pulled his grip away from the limb. Was that what happened to Haley? An overpowering tug. His legs curled around the trunk of the tree on the other side. He gripped the largest limb his hand could grasp, straddled the trunk and pulled himself upright, coughing and gasping for air.

Blake held on to a limb with his head pressed against the trunk. "We will find her, we will." His tone wasn't convincing. "She must have been swept downstream."

"Agreed. Let's get to the shore and start searching." Kendall stood and walked the length of the fallen tree, holding on to partially burned branches that extended into the air.

He reached dry, charred ground and paused in front of the men. Despite the constant sounds of the fire crackling, silence fell among them.

"The strong current must have pulled her under the tree somehow," Kendall announced to the other three men. He bent, placed his hands on his knees and ducked his head. Guilt over not protecting her better twisted in his gut. He wiped his tear-filled eyes.

God, please don't take her from me. Let me find her. Show me the way.

Blake, Mac, Connor and J.R. stood motionless, staring toward the water. Their solemn expressions spoke for them. Kendall's insides ripped with loss. He sucked in a deep breath and straightened.

"We can't give up." He traipsed along the shoreline with all four men on his heels. "We must believe God spared her. Keep your eyes open."

"You've got it." Blake caught up with Kendall. "She's stronger than you think. I grew up with her, so I know how tough she is."

Blake's attempt at positive thinking fell to the pit of Kendall's stomach. If Kendall looked at the situation from the physical point of view, she'd already drowned. The strength of powerful undertows could take down the strongest of men. It swept him off his feet, but he caught hold of a limb. In Haley's weakened state, only God could save her now.

Chapter Eleven

Haley spiraled downstream. Her legs, arms and body bumped against the debris floating around her. Thoughts of her parents' irresolvable grief flashed. Fear of drowning and never seeing them or Kendall again shot adrenaline into overdrive.

Lord, don't let me die.

The current swirled different directions, taking her body every which way. She gulped a mouthful of water an instant before her head bobbed out of the water. She spewed the water and gasped for air before being sucked back down. Her chest hurt and the ache in her throat forced her to cough underwater, losing her last breath.

A powerful thrust of rushing river pushed her farther away from Kendall. Would he be able to save her like he had before? A sudden shift in the current shoved her sideways. Her foot found the riverbed and her head emerged from the water. She gasped for breath and coughed until her throat and chest hurt. She could breathe.

Her muscles grew weary as she fought against the current, plodded her way to shore and fell on her knees. Tears flowed. Her hands covered her face. Sobs bellowed from the depths of her soul. She'd survived the turbulent river mere yards before the waters dropped over another steep waterfall.

Thank You, Lord.

How could this happen twice? She should've learned her lesson the first time. She'd held on to the small limbs of that fallen tree until they snapped. Her lifeline wasn't strong enough to hold her weight. Kendall dropped underwater right before her. Had he survived or was he swept away, too? Could he be somewhere close?

She studied her surroundings and stared at the river. Would she spot Kendall's body floating downstream? No. She couldn't think that way. He had to have survived. They were supposed to go out to dinner after this nightmare.

Her strength waned and her body trembled. She steadied her shaky legs and pushed to her feet. The densely populated forest held an eerie aura while thick smoke floated between the trees like low-lying clouds. Chills crawled over her arms and legs. Cold? No. Something wasn't right.

"Kendall." Her voice hung heavy in the air. "Kendall. Blake."

No response.

Where was she, and what was that humming roar?

Another firestorm? Kendall would know if he were there. Lightning flashed and flames exploded. She startled and dropped to her knees. Smoke thickened and billowed toward her. Her weakened muscles tensed. She couldn't run from the intense heat and the flames boiling toward her.

Her eyes shot back to the river. It was her only refuge. Drown or burn? She searched for something strong enough to keep her from washing away again.

Haley forced herself to her feet and stumbled toward another fallen tree. This one had been uprooted and lay partly in the river. Surprised the sandals still clung to her feet, she tightened the straps as tight as they would go, slid into the cold water and held on to large limbs with shaky hands. Her fingers whitened with her tight grip. Her feet lifted off the river floor, but the tree kept her from being whisked away. She shuffled her grip to another thick branch until both hands were underwater.

One glance back confirmed the fast-approaching flames. She sucked in a deep breath and ducked underwater. Heat from the blaze stirred on the surface above her. No doubt the fire raged overhead. How long could she hold her breath? She recalled Kendall's previous instructions and started counting down the seconds.

Her chest cramped and her stomach muscles tightened from the lack of oxygen. She pushed herself deeper and shifted under the half-submerged tree and up on the other side. Maybe she could grab a breath at the edge of its trunk. It mortified her that she'd burn if she surfaced and yet she was horrified that she'd drown if she didn't find air.

Haley tilted her face upward and inched her mouth to the surface. Water sloshed, and she gulped water. She coughed and spat. The rough tree scraped her cheek. With a quick gasp, air hit her lungs. Smoky air, but at least it held oxygen.

Seconds felt like hours. How long should she stay there? A burning branch fell from the nearby tree and barely missed her. The heat intensified while its fall leaves succumbed to the flames and curled around the edges.

What were the chances another limb would fall? She took another breath and shuffled back to the other side of the tree trunk and braved lifting her head completely out into the open. Warmth hit her face, but it was bearable. Her hands felt around for more branches to help get her to the shore.

Haley's wet clothes clung to her body. Water rolled and dripped from her hair. For a moment, the heat warmed her chilled skin before it switched over to the heat of a midsummer day. Still bearable. She pushed the hair off her face and wiped her eyes. Her vision cleared.

The forest burned around her, but not as intense as what she'd experienced. She straightened, intent on finding Kendall. Her best option was to head back upstream. She'd walk the shoreline. Surely Kendall and the escapees would head downstream in search of her. Or had they given up? She had to believe they were looking for her. If Kendall was the man she'd grown to admire, he would never give up.

Haley stepped over the charred ground cover. She checked her sandals to see if they were melting. The pungent smell of burning rubber assaulted her nose. She stepped into the icy river to cool them off. No one would ever believe she'd been in a forest fire and survived wearing men's rubber sandals. She could barely believe it herself.

"I can do this," she mumbled as she surveyed her surroundings. The thought of being alone would never hold the same meaning. Being alone at home, reading a book or relaxing in the peace and quiet was therapeutic and restful. However, standing alone in the middle of nowhere, amid a life-threatening situation with very little food or water, no sense of direction or any way to protect herself became isolation.

A half-burned limb lay on the ground. She picked it up and held it in the unburned portion. If it didn't fall apart, it was the perfect size to use as a hiking stick. With a thrust to its tip into the ground, she tested the strength. It held up. Satisfied, she began a careful trek upstream with occasional dips of her feet in the water to cool her sandals. Trepidation crept over her at the what-ifs.

What if she didn't find Kendall? What if wild animals returned or were hiding, waiting to pounce on her? What if she starved to death or passed out from the lack of proper hydration?

Stop it. I refuse to think negatively. Lord, You said I can do all things through the strength You give me.

You said You'd never leave me. Therefore, I'm not alone. You're walking this forest with me. I choose to believe You.

Maybe if she kept calling out to Kendall or Blake, they'd hear her. Each step forward was a step closer toward them, she reasoned.

"K-e-n-d-a-l-l," she yelled. "B-l-a-k-e."

The forest fell quiet with occasional crackling and the sound of a branch or tree falling. Smoke and the stifling smell of smoldering debris kept her focusing on how deeply she breathed. She ducked her face into her T-shirt for a moment and took in a deep breath, pushing forward through some tall, undamaged weeds.

Her thoughts drifted to the value of life, her parents, Kendall and her envisioned future. Life truly was short. Seems it was only yesterday she and Blake were racing to see who could climb to the top of a tree faster. How had he changed so? Her parents always made sure she had what she needed. Maybe not everything she wanted, but she had no actual needs, and that was a blessing. Kendall was another story. A knight in shining armor, as the old saying goes. He'd put his life on the line and saved her multiple times. Could he ever see himself with her?

"K-e-n-d-a-l-l." She waited. No response. "B-l-a-k-e."

Her mouth grew dry. Silly with a river flowing beside her. If she became too parched, she'd give in and moisten her mouth with river water. She'd read about all the germs and vowed never to take a sip, but that could change.

Despite the dangers she'd encountered during her supposed vacation, Haley found she loved the mountains, the forest and the beauty of its rivers and rock formations—even the wild animals. Well, as long as none of them reappeared and came after her. With no job to report back to, it might be nice to live in a small town close to nature. Certainly, there were dental offices in less populated areas like this that would need a dental assistant. The thought brought a smile to her face.

Her foot slipped on some rocks, and she stumbled forward. Best to keep her eyes open and her mind focused on where she stepped and what lay before her.

The dense forest cast dark shadows on the ground. What time was it? Had the day gone by, and darkness was about to consume her? A loud pop had her searching for the source. She looked up in time to spot a large limb falling overhead. Her sandal slipped in the mud. She lost her footing and fell face-first. A horrified scream spewed from her lips. It felt like her whole body was stinging, especially her sore arm. Had the tree limbs stabbed her multiple times? Was she about to die?

Her heart thrashed against her chest. She lifted her head and spat mud and debris from her mouth. No shooting pain and she could still breathe. The large limb hadn't pulverized her. Haley evaluated her predicament as best as she could. One end of the branch caught on a low-lying branch in another tree.

The heavier end landed on a boulder just high enough to not press her deeper into the ground. Still, the smaller limbs pinned her down. If either end slipped, well, she couldn't think about what might happen.

Her fingers wiggled with no pain. Mud squished between them. One arm remained unharmed and free. The mud-covered gunshot wound burned. She blew on it, but it didn't help the sting. Stubs of thicker branches pressed against her other arm and legs. Her back ached slightly. At least it hadn't pressed her into the ground and cut off her breathing or crushed her completely.

Any efforts to free herself turned futile. Her strength waned. If she rested a minute, could she use her one free hand to dig beneath her so her body would drop enough for her to shimmy out from under the limb? Doubtful. She bent her free arm and rested her cheek on her forearm.

Her thoughts went different directions. Tears wouldn't help. If she yelled too much, maybe it would attract the wildlife and they'd consider her an easy meal. Should she remain quiet and listen for Kendall's voice, and take the risk of not being found?

A slight rustling at her feet sent her pulse into overdrive. If whatever was causing the sound was human, they would have spoken and helped her. She froze and focused on breathing, quiet and slow. Anticipation of sharp teeth clamping into her calves prickled the hair on her neck while a scream crept into her vocal cords, ready to release. She pressed her lips together and held it back. Fear of the unexpected threatened a panic attack.

Light movement shuffled around the fallen limb. Her eyes searched for a visual of the animal. More movement drew close. Brown fur, slender, long legs. A head with antlers dipped to the ground. It was a buck. Another deer appeared in the distance. She relaxed and blew out a breath. The buck bolted from her slight movement.

Lord, please don't let Kendall and Blake give up on me. Protect me and give me wisdom and strength to figure out how to free myself. I don't want to be stuck out here in the pitch black.

Kendall stiffened and sucked in a deep breath. He had recognized the thunder and the sound a fire makes when it's angry. Whether it was a fire swirl or a firestorm that rolled by, he could only pray Haley had made it to a safe place.

Time was wasting and the sun was about to set. They had to hurry down the riverbank and watch for signs of her before it got too dark. Thoughts and regrets swirled through his head. He'd never regret becoming a Forest Service firefighter. It was an honor and a pleasure to hold such a title. That was the one thing he was certain about. But he did regret how he acted toward Haley earlier. It wasn't her fault he was falling for her and didn't know what to do about it. And he did regret what had happened between him and his dad.

Who knew he would become so angry the day

Kendall told him he didn't want to pursue a career in welding? The family business was the perfect opportunity for someone with the skills and drive to continue making it successful. He'd helped his dad many times, but always knew it wasn't for him. His dad's rejection was unexpected and painful. His ex-girlfriend, whom he thought would be his forever bride, argued and demanded he select a safer profession, or she'd walk away. And walk away she did.

Why had those he loved tried to plan his life for him? Why couldn't they understand he loved forestry, and this is where he belonged? If he hadn't become a firefighter, would someone else have found Haley tied up and gagged in that cabin, or would she have died there? Was this God's way of placing the genuine love of his life in his path?

Firefighting seeped into his blood early on when he witnessed firefighters saving his parents' home at the edge of the forest in the mountain valley after it had been struck by lightning. He decided as a kid to become a firefighter and help save others' homes and lives in the area, too. Every time Kendall talked about it growing up, his dad became disgruntled and insisted he stay with the family business where it's safe. He'd reminded Kendall of the dangers of firefighting, and that he should run from fires rather than toward them.

The constant reminder of the family's near-death fire encounter had the opposite effect on him than his dad intended. Kendall's desire to help others and save the forest only intensified. He had dropped the subject until he turned eighteen and it was time to get a job. Then he officially turned down his dad's job offer and was hired by the forestry service. Things hadn't been the same between them since.

Haley seemed to understand his passion. At least, he'd like to think her interest wasn't just because he'd saved her. Her kind and encouraging words about his job had sparked his interest in her.

A stick broke under his foot. He glanced down at his boot, and it occurred to him that if Haley survived, the sandals probably didn't. If that were the case, she'd be out there walking barefooted through the thickness, which would be slow going and would burn her feet.

"H-a-l-e-y." Kendall paused, listened and observed the area. He longed to hear her respond. His insides twisted not knowing her whereabouts or if she was hurt.

Blake cupped his hands around his mouth. "H-a-l-e-y."

The other men began calling her name.

Kendall threw his hand in the air. "Quiet. If she yells back, we need to hear her."

"No way could she survive those rapids," Connor said.

Blake shoved a finger toward Connor. "Don't talk like that. She's gonna make it."

"Whatever." Connor traipsed ahead of everyone else. "You guys are holding on to lost hope."

Kendall waved off Connor's negative attitude. Some people just didn't get it. He'd seen people survive incredible situations that should have killed them. If he knew Haley like he thought, banking on Blake's words, she was a fighter and didn't give up easily. He picked up the pace and trekked down the mountain.

"You like my cousin, don't you?" Blake stepped up beside Kendall.

"The question is, do *you* like your cousin? Is that why you left her to die?" Kendall bit his lip. He should remain professional, but Blake had used Haley and showed no remorse for the harm that could have come to her. "Are you saying you care about her now?"

"Guess I deserve your attitude. I haven't made the best choices in the past few years, but Haley was always the kindhearted, faithful sort. She deserves better, and I failed her." Blake swiped his hand over his face. "I'm glad you rescued her and saved her life. No thanks to me or my friends."

Kendall wasn't sure how Blake could consider the escapees his friends. They'd dump him in a heartbeat if it came down to who would survive.

"I can tell you like her. I saw you kiss her back at the waterfall." Blake's eyebrows lifted.

"I don't know her that well, but I like what I see, and I like her positive attitude. She comes across as trustworthy and caring. Seems to have a strong faith in God." Kendall glanced around the forest and back at the debris floating in the water. "She could be out there floating downstream holding on to one of those logs."

"For the record, she is true-blue, as they say, and yes, she's always been a church girl. As much as I fight against what she believes, I know in my gut she's right. But I'm damaged goods now that I have a record. God probably won't be of any help to me now." Blake picked up a rock and tossed it into the water as they walked.

Damaged goods. Kendall hadn't looked at his situation with his dad as damaged, and yet, that's exactly what it was. "After listening to Haley all this time, no one is too messed up to be saved by God. Damaged or not, we're all the same."

"What do you think?" Blake's serious tone put Kendall on the spot.

What he thought now was different from what he thought even a few days ago. He'd been wrong to compare his dad's attitude and behavior to God.

Could He help him reconcile his differences with his dad? "I think God can do anything with anyone regardless of their past if they are willing to admit their sins and repent of them. Hmm, now I'm sounding like Haley."

"I like the idea." Blake pushed a charred limb aside.

"What are y'all yapping about up there?" J.R.'s voice fell flat. "If you ask me, the girl is halfway to Chattanooga by now, assuming that river goes that far."

"Nobody asked your opinion." Blake tossed the Pulaski into his other hand.

"I still have a weapon, you know."

Kendall shook his head. Were all prisoners this argumentative? Such wasted energy. Too bad they didn't devote themselves to a worthwhile job like fighting fires and respecting the lives of others, protecting and salvaging the land.

"Look. What's that?" Mac pointed to something in the water.

Kendall dived in first. Blake followed. Before he knew it, all the men were swimming toward a log, except for Connor who stood on the bank. Something that looked like hair bobbing in the water was on the other side. Could it be Haley? He wanted it to be her, but if it was, she wasn't responding.

As they swam closer, a squirrel jumped to another log and onto the shore. He skittered along the ground and scurried away.

"Too bad. Thought we had something." Mac flipped over and swam toward the shore.

"The rapids are much stronger here." Kendall fought against the swift waters to get to the shore. Disappointment loomed. He'd doubted it was her hanging on to that log. Seemed a little too coincidental. His eyes lifted to the sky.

Where is she?

"H-a-l-e-y." He drew her name out and listened for a response.

A different type of rumbling noise caught his attention. He swirled in time to see several boulders rolling downhill toward them.

"Get out of the way. Falling rocks." Kendall dived for an open space in the trees. His knee hit a stump and a pain shot through his leg. He flipped over and jerked his feet up just in time. One of the boulders almost scraped his side. *That was close, too close.*

An enormous stone followed by three smaller ones tumbled past them.

"Whoa," J.R. yelled from the distance. "Almost got me."

One rock slammed into a tree. The burned tree cracked, and the top collapsed to the ground. Flames shot out from inside the trunk.

Blake ran in the opposite direction. "This is like a war zone, and we're under attack."

"Feels like it." Kendall hopped to his feet too fast. Pain shot through his knee. He clenched his teeth and massaged the ache away. He'd have to go easy on that leg to make sure he hadn't pulled something or torn a ligament.

"I thought all those signs along the road, warning people of falling rocks, were to keep people on their toes and obedient to the forestry rules." Mac put a twig in his mouth and chewed on it.

"There's nothing to joke about. There's lots of dangers here. You either love it or hate it. The mountains are safe if you do your part and respect how nature works." Kendall proceeded on his journey with a slight limp. "Watch behind you. Where there are falling rocks, there could be more behind them."

"Are you trying to keep us on edge?" Blake jammed the Pulaski into the ground. "We need to keep searching for my cousin."

Everyone quieted. Kendall eyed the guys, who

thought they were so tough. Losing Haley had affected them all. Even if they hadn't admitted it, she'd made a positive impression on each one. Especially her cousin, whose attitude had changed the most.

"I need water and something to eat," Connor said.

"Don't you have the bottled water J.R. gave you?" Mac kicked at a smoldering bush.

"I drank it." Connor threw his hands in the air.

"Quit your whining," Blake responded. "You were supposed to take sips, not gulp it."

"It's your fault we're in this mess." J.R. stepped to the edge of the water. "The jail break was your idea."

"Well, no one made you help us." Blake's face reddened.

"Connor did. Said it would be the challenge of my life. Dumbest decision I ever made, listening to a convict. I could be home right now eating anything I want." J.R.'s comment held regret. "Now my career is over, and I've earned jail time."

"Hey." Mac kept walking. "Look on the bright side. We could be cellmates."

Kendall strained to hear noises in the woods. Other than the occasional popping, sizzling or the swoosh of a tree hitting the ground, he hadn't heard what he longed for. Haley's voice calling out to him. He swallowed hard. He wondered if she'd kept any of the survival information he'd shared in the short time they'd been together. She could survive. He refused to allow doubt into his thoughts.

"H-a-l-e-y," he called out repeatedly. "Where are you?"

He pushed some limbs aside and came to a sudden halt.

"What is it?" Blake stood in front of him.

"Quiet. Thought I heard something." Kendall held his arm out.

Connor huffed.

Kendall called out to her again. "H-a-l-e-y."

A faint sound came from the distance. Could it be her? He took off running despite the ache in his knee. Blake remained close beside him. His long legs stretched out faster than Kendall's. The others were somewhere behind him. His pulse raced to the beat of a repeater rifle. He shoved limbs away from his face and kept his focus straight ahead.

He ran about the length of a football field, paused and yelled again.

"H-a-l-e-y."

"K-e-n-d-a-l-l." Her voice was still distant. She was alive. He continued running until he'd reached another assumed length of a football field and called again.

"Where are you?" He expected an answer, but there was no response.

"Where do you think she is, or was it a fluke? Maybe we imagined it." Connor's constant doubting annoyed Kendall.

"K-e-n-d-a-l-l." The sound of her voice became clearer.

They were close, but where was she? He walked faster, searching for movement. Had she fallen into another ravine or into a hole somewhere? He paused and studied the forest before him. Movement under a large fallen limb caught his attention.

"Haley. Is that you?" His heart thrashed against his chest.

"Help me. I'm stuck." Her weak voice shot concern through him.

He took off running. Blake bypassed him as they both raced toward her.

"I think I'm okay, just pinned down." Haley's smile shone like a spotlight on her muddy face.

"Come on, guys, let's get this limb off of her." Kendall remained close to Haley. The other four spaced out, lifted the heavy branch and set it aside. He helped her up.

"You found me." She pushed to her feet, jumped into his arms, mud and all, and squeezed. "I prayed I wouldn't have to lie there all night. Thank you, all of you, for rescuing me."

It was all he could do to keep from planting a kiss on those parched lips. He caved when her big brown, thankful eyes searched his face. He took the tail of his shirt and wiped mud from her face, then gave her a quick kiss. They'd found her and that's all that mattered.

"We've been looking for you." Leave it to Mac to squelch a memorable moment. At least no one had commented on the kiss.

"Thought you'd never find me. What an answer to prayer." Her excited tone was like music to Kendall's ears. "At one point I thought a wild animal was going to attack, but it turned out to be a buck and a doe. I was so relieved."

Her smile and exuberance were far different from the response Kendall expected. She'd been swept downstream, almost drowned, pinned down by an extra large limb, and yet here she stood excited, like she'd just gotten off a roller coaster. She didn't complain.

Blake stepped over and drew her in for a hug. "I'm glad you're safe, cuz. I would have blamed myself if anything happened to you."

"It was quite frightening. The current was worse than the one Kendall and I experienced the other day. I managed to grab hold of a tree that had fallen across the river and pulled myself out." Her focus turned to Kendall. "Then I heard a roar and spotted a ball of fire headed straight toward me. I remembered what Kendall taught us. Take a deep breath and duck underwater, then count. I spotted an uprooted tree half in the river and nervously slipped back into the water and submerged myself. Then I slowly emerged face up to catch a breath. It was intense, but I survived."

"So proud of you and your courage." Kendall put his arm around her shoulders and gave her a side hug.

"Now that you've saved me again and everyone is safe, I'm great." Haley turned the direction she'd just come from and pointed to the river. "Let me wash off some of this mud and we can continue our journey."

Kendall and the rest of the guys walked with her to the edge of the river. She looked over her shoulder at him and held out her hand. Kendall stopped, realizing he was hovering over her. He backed away.

"No worries. I'm not getting in the water. I've had enough of undercurrents." She rinsed her hands, then splashed water on her face, neck and arms until the mud cleared.

"Don't worry about your clothes." Kendall stepped closer. "Once it dries, it will be easier to crumble off."

"Good idea." She backed away from the river. "I lost my water bottle."

Kendall handed over his bottle. She sipped a couple of drinks and handed it back.

"Glad she's okay, but we need to get moving. We've wasted time already." Mac walked away. "Come on, Connor. Let's go."

Kendall took Haley's hand. "Ready?"

"Definitely." Her hand fit into his hand even better than before. He clasped his hand around her slender fingers. "Let's go."

Kendall found himself speechless. All he could do was thank God for sparing her.

It was as though she'd found a new spurt of energy or she'd gulped an energy drink. She still wore his sandals, and yet there was a bounce in each of her steps. Emotions played a huge role in survival. She'd been through a traumatic experience. Kendall squeezed her hand slightly.

Her eyebrows lifted and she squeezed his hand, too.

"I prayed for God's help, and He sent you again." She pushed hair from her face.

"I prayed, too." Kendall suddenly realized God had answered both of their prayers. A warmth flooded his heart.

Haley tilted her head and looked to the sky. "Awesome. This is miraculous. Otherwise, I would have tumbled over that huge waterfall." The sparkle in her eyes did his heart good.

He mulled over her words. He loved God but hadn't truly considered that God was everywhere, all the time, and He was listening. The weight of loss lifted from his shoulders. Responsibility set in. Now it was time to get them to safety before they all dehydrated or starved. Could they make it before dark?

Chapter Twelve

Haley was beside herself with joy and relief that God had answered her prayers and led Kendall and the escapees to her location. All wasn't lost. She'd survived a horrific ordeal and discovered a newfound depth to her faith.

Kendall appeared happy to see her, and the rest of the guys looked shocked and relieved she'd made it, especially Blake. His demeanor had changed for the better in the short time they'd been separated. Now to keep morale up so they could find their way out of the burning forest.

"We'll have to walk the scorched ground the rest of the way." Kendall pulled out his wet map. "We're not jumping in any more rivers."

"Great idea. I'm staying away from swirling waters." She remained by his side. The others moved in behind her to see the map. Kendall's finger moved across the map to a place that showed two waterways merging into the Blue Ridge Mountain Forest. His finger then circled until he spotted a location that mirrored where they stood.

"I believe this is where we are. It looks like more forest ahead, then a small meadow and more trees. There's a highway beyond that last set of trees if we can get that far. I'm hoping the fire has moved more to the west since we're heading northwest." He folded the paper and stuffed it back into his pack. "If we follow the river until it curves, then we'll be on the right track. My best guess is we are about three miles from our destination."

"Three miles," Blake repeated. "That doesn't sound bad." He clapped his hands together. "Let's get going. I'm hungry and thirsty, and there's food at the end of this journey."

"You're quite the cheerleader today." Haley followed behind Kendall.

"Better than complaining," Blake said. "We're all alive."

About time someone realized complaining wouldn't do them any good. Haley smiled at the change in Blake's attitude. Kendall's hand reached out for hers and she gladly took it again.

"It's getting dark. We may need to stop and build a campfire, then keep going in the morning." Kendall stepped over several large rocks embedded in the ground and pointed them out to her. "I've said it before. It's dangerous to hike through the forest in the dark."

"I agree, and I'm thankful none of us have broken any bones. Someone could get hurt on this uneven,

rocky ground. Watch out for those tree roots, too."
She made sure her feet landed firmly as she walked
beside Kendall. He kept a tight grip on her hand and
steadied her.

"I'm ready to get out of here. I don't care if it is
dark." Connor high-stepped it over a moss-covered
rock.

"What about the rest of you?" Kendall asked.
"Who wants to continue at dawn?"

"We're so close." Blake stepped beside Kendall.
"However, I like having a visual of where I'm going
and what's under my feet. I don't think there are
snakes in the burned soil this time of year, but I sure
don't want to find out the hard way that I'm wrong."

"True, and it could take twice the time to get there
in the dark."

"Hadn't thought about that." Mac joined them.

Kendall stopped and pulled out his flashlight. He
lit up the area in front of them. "This looks like a
good place to stop. Obviously, we're exposed to the
elements this time, but at first light, we can make
our way to the possible rescue zone in a shorter time.
You're right, Blake. It's ludicrous to risk the uneven
terrain after dark."

"Guess that means we find a log or rock or tree
to lean on until morning." Haley must reel in her
adrenaline and try resting. Not sure the excitement
of sleeping in her own bed tomorrow night would
let her sleep tonight.

"Exactly." Mac plopped on the ground and leaned
against a tree.

Connor huffed and sat on the ground.

"Nobody helping build a fire?" Kendall tossed what sticks he could find on the ground. Most of them were scorched. "It's important to our safety out here in the wild for us to have a campfire and stay in close proximity to the flames."

"Here's a few more." Blake dropped the sticks and dried moss he'd found. Connor tossed his cigarette lighter over to Blake to start the fire. In a matter of seconds, a small flame grew into larger ones.

"Think I'll dig a small fire line around our campfire." Kendall poked and arranged the sticks and cleared a circle around the blaze to keep it from spreading, not that the previous blaze hadn't already done its damage to the area. At least he'd located a couple of small crevasses that had trapped some short sticks and dried leaves.

"I still say it's weird to start a fire when we're running from one." Connor lay back on the ground with one arm bent at the elbow, resting his forearm on his forehead.

"It does sound ridiculous, but even in fighting wildfires, we sometimes purposely burn some of the terrain in an attempt to stop the crawling flames from going any farther. Funny how it all works, but it does." Kendall stood and put his hands at his waist. He turned slowly. As far as Haley could tell, he studied their surroundings until their eyes met and he smiled at her.

Haley sat by a log and stretched her legs. She admired Kendall's protective nature. He walked over and joined her. He put his arm around her shoulders. Such a comforting feeling. Kind of like a warm blanket on a chilly night. She laid her head against his chest and stared into the campfire. They were sitting ducks for whatever wildlife was brave enough to come close.

Blake sat in front of the flame. "I'll take first watch." He broke a stick in little pieces and tossed them one by one into the fire.

Haley wondered what was on Blake's mind. Regret, maybe. She blew out a slow breath and closed her eyes, but her thoughts wouldn't shut down. The convicts' snores increased until they overpowered the sound of the rushing river not far from them. Blake had softened his hostile behavior. He was different somehow. She liked the change.

Connor, J.R. and Mac, well, she hadn't quite figured them out. Kendall, on the other hand, had captured her heart without trying.

A thin cloud of smoke hung overhead, and she could still hear the occasional crackling sounds of wood burning. A howl in the distance didn't bother her until several other howls and barks followed. Were those coyotes coming for them? Fear gripped her and her pulse raced.

Kendall sat up. The barking grew closer. "Sounds like coyotes. Everybody, stand up and move closer to the fire. Grab some rocks or sticks to throw at them if they come this way. The idea is to scare them, not injure them. They aren't usually dangerous to humans, but we don't want to underestimate their mood."

"So, they won't attack us?" Haley scooped up a few small rocks.

"Attacks on humans are extremely rare." Kendall pulled out his flashlight. "I've been told they don't like flashing lights or loud noises. If they stop to check us out, yell at them."

"Oh, I can yell. Believe me," Connor said. "I've got my gun, too."

"Don't shoot them. If you must, then shoot in the air." Kendall shined his flashlight all around their campsite and out into the forest depths. "I don't see anything. Wait. There."

Barking, growling and yelping grew closer. A pack of white eyes glowed in the dark and stared back at them. Haley tensed and drew in a shaky breath. Everyone threw their rocks in the coyotes' direction. Then, in a flash, as quick as they'd appeared, they pushed back and ran deep into the forest until the sound of their howls and barks finally faded. Haley released the breath she'd held. They weren't after them at all. A few minutes later, the coyote howls faded into the silence.

"All's clear. You can lie back down." Kendall sat by the fire. "We survived that pack of coyotes."

"You say that like any of us could sleep right now." Blake sat opposite Kendall.

"Well, I'm staying by you guys." Haley plopped on the ground and crossed her legs. "I'm wide awake. Guess we will sit here until daylight."

The night was long, but she'd rather lose a little sleep than be caught off guard by approaching animals. Blake and his friends drifted off to sleep. Kendall drew in the blackened ground with a stick.

Sunrise hadn't come soon enough. The roar of the river sang in tune with the sound of the burning forest. A grim reminder they weren't out of danger yet.

Haley stood and stretched. Kendall did likewise. He kicked dirt over the fire, which seemed ironic considering their situation. But he was a firefighter, and she guessed it came naturally, like back at the cave.

"Time to go. Everybody up," Kendall said.

Haley observed the lazy body language of the escapees as they rolled flat on their backs and stretched before jumping to their feet. In a matter of minutes, they were all trekking the mountain again.

"Keep your eyes open on all these burned trees. Notice the way they're entangled with each other while more broken limbs dangle and are threatening to fall at any moment." Kendall's warning only reminded her of the dangers of the forest she'd experienced firsthand, especially after a fire.

Her socks were black with soot and ashes. The river might have cleaned them some, but after traipsing through the forest, they dirtied up all over again. At least she still wore the battered sandals.

"Do you think your handcrew knows where you are or where we are? You said they were looking for us?" Haley asked.

"It's possible they may be somewhere near the meadow, but it all still depends on…"

"On the wind and the perimeters of the fire."

Haley tossed her hands in the air and laughed. "I know. You've ingrained that into my mind."

"Yes, and each time the answer is always the same." Kendall pushed a half-burned limb aside to keep from running into it. He held it back for her. "Doesn't look like the fire totally wiped out this area. Things look good right now."

Connor drifted out to the right of them. Haley learned from being by Kendall's side that he preferred they all stay closer together. He'd warned them multiple times.

Connor picked up a stick and hit it against a tree. He stepped on top of a log and hopped off, then used his stick as a cane. He jabbed it into the ground and moved farther away.

"Hey, the ground is smoother out here. Y'all should join me." His snarky demeanor switched to a more jovial tone. "Only three more miles." Connor jumped in the air and kicked his heels together, then landed in an awkward position.

Haley sucked in a breath as she watched him fall. He yelled and rolled on the ground holding his leg. She ran with Kendall and the others and stood over Connor. "Looks like you've broken your ankle."

"You don't have to tell me." Connor held his leg and moaned. His gleeful attitude had disappeared.

Kendall touched her arm and looked around. "We need to find something to make a temporary splint."

Everyone, except Connor, searched the forest for sticks straight enough to use on Connor's ankle.

"Here are two that might work." J.R. held two short sticks in the air.

"Yes, those will work." Kendall took them and placed them on the ground. He pulled his rope from his fire pack. "Anyone have a knife?"

The men emptied their pockets. "Do we look like we're equipped with knives?"

J.R. held out a pocketknife. "I have one."

"Leave it to the prison guard to have another weapon." Mac found another twig to chew on.

Haley leaned in to help Kendall splint Connor's ankle, and they bumped heads. They exchanged a glance. She froze, not wanting to interrupt the surreal moment of his closeness, as the connection between them mounted.

"Haley." Kendall's voice drew her focus back to the present.

"What?" She met his gaze, almost nose to nose. Those intense eyes messed with her emotions. He was close enough to kiss again. Close enough to confirm everything was going to be okay.

"You can let go." He nodded at her hands still holding the sticks in place. "I need to tie the rope, and your hand is in the way."

"Oh." She jerked her arm out of the way, stepped back and gave him plenty of room to work. Her wounded arm throbbed after the sudden movement. Three miles. Would the rescue team find them? Would they have plenty of food and water? Three more miles and she'd find out if Kendall's interest in her would extend beyond the forest fire.

"Can he walk?" Mac asked.

Blake let out a huff. "Are you seriously asking that question? You can tell from the looks of that break that we will have to carry him out of here."

"That's gonna slow us down, big-time." J.R. kicked at a rock and almost fell over.

"Yep, and if you break your ankle, I'm not carrying you, so toughen up, big guy, and lend a hand. We can take turns." Blake punched J.R.'s arm and grinned. "We've only got three miles. That'll be a breeze."

Kendall handed J.R. his pocketknife, then rolled up the rest of his rope and placed it back in his pack. Haley's stomach rumbled. Everyone turned and looked at her.

"What can I say? I'm hungry." She held her hands in the air.

"We all are, and if we have to stay here another night, I'm going hunting. We need something to eat and some water. I don't plan to starve to death." Mac rubbed his forehead before helping Connor up on his one foot. "Besides, I've got a killer headache."

"The altitude can mess with you," Kendall said. "In this elevation, you need water to help with oxygen intake. Let's get moving."

"I'll follow everyone and help whenever I'm needed." Haley's nurturing instinct kicked in, and she needed to make sure Connor was okay. She dropped back behind all the guys.

"I'd rather you stay up here with me so I can watch after you. Those guys can take care of themselves."

Kendall eyed her. "If we run into trouble, I'd rather you be close to me." He motioned for her to step forward.

Haley complied with his request, happy that he wanted her close. She stepped over a large tree root and fell in line behind him.

A grin slid across his face and the look in his eyes softened. "Good. Thank you."

Even though she wasn't sure where their relationship would go from here, being near him comforted her. They traipsed through the burned underbrush. The blaze had devoured most of the vegetation but hadn't affected their thorny sharpness. Thorns dug into her lounge pants and tugged at her T-shirt. Smoke lingered in the air like a heavy fog. Each breath inhaled a measure of the thickness and mixed with the musty odor of burned wood.

Blake and J.R. stood on each side of Connor and interlocked arms. Connor moaned with movement. There wasn't anything Haley could do to make his pain subside but pray.

Lord, You've brought us this far and You've taken care of us. Please let the rescue team find us before we are too weak to keep moving. And would You help Connor? He's in a lot of pain.

Some trees still blazed above their heads and stretched out into the surrounding distance. Flames still devoured areas of the underbrush. Thankfully, the loud roar of the fire had subsided. Maybe it was quiet because the wind wasn't blowing much.

Her thoughts drifted. How were her parents

doing? Would her moving away affect them negatively? Settling in a small town sounded peaceful and pleasant. Was her friend feeling better now? What about Kendall? He'd stepped into her life, and she couldn't imagine going on without him.

Smoke blew in her face. She blinked her eyes and focused on keeping in step with him and adding an occasional jog to catch up with his long stride. How he'd maintained a positive attitude throughout their trauma, she did not know. His honesty proved he was a man of integrity. She couldn't help but like the guy. He'd kept them from panicking at the worst, most frightening times.

A fiery branch plummeted to the ground off in the distance. The swoosh and cracking branches captured her attention. She glanced overhead. Would limbs crash down on them?

"Ohhhh, how-much far-ther?" Connor's moaning stutter was a sure sign he needed something for pain. His cries fell flat in the decimated forest, leaving the rest of them to deal with the sound of agony.

"What time is it? Should be about midnight, if you ask me." Mac's weary voice reached Haley's ears. "I didn't sleep a wink."

Kendall paused and glanced into the sky, then proceeded hiking. "My guess is it's somewhere around noon."

"Then we should make the clearing today," Haley said, wiping her sweaty palms on her filthy lounge pants. Some of the half-dried mud fell off. She wiped at the dirt on her T-shirt and a few clumps fell. Her hair had dried some, too, and hung in matted ringlets around her face.

"I'm counting on it." Kendall pushed past several low-hanging limbs. He held them back for her. "Don't let this smack you in the face. It's a poison sumac tree. If you're allergic to poison ivy and poison oak, you're probably allergic to sumac."

"I am. On all three counts." Haley ducked under the branch while Kendall held it. "My grandparents had the trio on their property when I was younger. Blake and I stumbled right into it when we were out exploring one weekend. I had to get shots before it would clear up, but he was basically fine."

She appreciated Kendall's thoughtfulness as he held the branch back for the criminals, too. They'd almost become friends after all they'd been through together. The police would probably be waiting whenever they're rescued. Too bad those guys made a decision that would keep them behind bars longer than their original sentences. Even Blake.

Her mouth grew dry, and her thigh and calf muscles threatened cramps. No sense complaining. Kendall had already shared a few sips of his nearly empty water bottle.

Whatever brand the sandals were, she'd notify the company and compliment them on how well they'd held up under the wilderness terrain. Who knew? They might want to do a commercial about the beating they took in a firestorm. At least she could still find a little humor in it all. They didn't shield her foot from pokes and scrapes, but they padded the bottom of her feet. Kendall's socks had threads pulled, several holes and a tear.

Thank You, Lord, for protecting my feet.

"What do you plan to do once you're rescued?" Kendall's voice broke into her private conversation with herself.

"Get a drink of water, wash my hands and face, call my parents, eat, shower, put on clean clothes, sleep in my bed." She scrolled through all the things she wanted to do. "Just to name a few."

"You covered the important stuff." Kendall offered a half-hearted chuckle. "My list is about the same, but I'll meet up with my handcrew and update them before I do much else."

"Will they let you rest? I mean, look at what we've been through. They don't expect you to jump right back into fighting the fire, do they?" She couldn't imagine going back to work without some downtime first.

"No, nothing like that." Kendall slowed. "Watch all these mangled tree roots."

She twisted her foot this way and that, then stepped on top of roots and over others. "That was a trap if I've ever seen one."

"Hey, slow down," Blake said. "We need to switch up carrying Connor."

"I gotcha." Mac took over for Blake. "You good?" he asked J.R.

"Still got a few steps in me." J.R. spat on the ground. "Don't want to slow down."

Kendall coughed. "I'll report to my team leaders, and they'll want me to go back to the command center for evaluation, nourishment and rest. They're a great bunch of guys. We look out for each other."

"Do you ever go into the city?" Would he come see her if she invited him? Better let well enough alone. If he was interested, he'd find a way to communicate. She should let God do His thing and bring the one He sees fit into her life. Kendall looked like a good choice.

"Not very often. Not unless there is something really special in the city."

Haley pondered his comment. Would she be that something?

Kendall sighed. How much longer would he last without food and water? He'd forewarned the rest of the group about their lack, but he wanted to get everyone to safety before they passed out from dehydration, including himself. Food was one thing, but the lack of adequate water could be deadly.

He stared into the thick, burning forest. Looks could be deceiving. Those flames could erupt like a volcano if the wind picked up and the atmospheric pressure was right. Were his eyes playing tricks on him? The clearing he'd spotted on the map. Was that it ahead? His heart thrashed against his chest as thoughts of drawing to the end of their nightmare bombarded his mind.

"Slow down, Kendall." Haley ran up behind him. "My legs aren't as long as yours. I'm about ready to collapse trying to keep the pace."

"My bad." Kendall stopped and waited for everyone to catch up. He didn't want to hear all the grumbling. Everyone was on edge, and rightly so. Haley, not so much, but the look in her eyes told him she'd had enough. She'd been a real trooper.

"Yeah, you're running off and leaving us." Perspiration rolled down Mac's forehead.

"Quiet." Kendall threw his hand in the air. Everyone hushed.

"What is it?" Haley's breathless whisper slipped through her parched lips.

"Sounds like a plane." He looked up, but the trees were too thick to see through. "Could be the smoke jumpers or sawyers."

"Really?" A sparkle shone in Haley's eyes. She looked at the same tree-filled sky. "I can't see it, but I think I hear it, too."

"I'm not going back to jail." Mac halted and looked around with his lips drawn tight.

"How far do you think you'll make it with no food or water?" Blake asked. "A day or two at the most."

"I'm with Mac. I'll take my chances." J.R.'s voice took a stern shift.

"What about me?" Connor straightened with one knee bent as he held his broken ankle off the ground.

"You can't run anywhere. Looks like you're going back to the hole," Mac said.

Blake brushed debris off his pants legs. "My trust is in this firefighter."

"Don't put your trust in me. Trust God. All of you. He's the one who brought us this far." Kendall shocked himself with his bold statement. Trust is what he'd missed in his relationship with God. He'd talked to Him several times lately, but he hadn't trusted God would follow through.

Just in the short time Kendall had been with Haley, she'd already made a difference in his life. He looked at his feet and kicked at several leaves and twigs on the ground, and whispered an inward prayer.

God, forgive me for not trusting You with my problems. I give them to You and trust that You are in control, and I trust You've sent rescuers.

"Kendall's right. If it weren't for God's protection and guidance, we wouldn't have made it this far. Faith the size of a mustard seed is all it takes, according to the Bible." Haley slapped at a bug flying around her head.

"We're not out of here yet and you're acting like this is the end of our journey." Blake flipped the Pulaski up and stuck it in the ground.

Kendall imagined what would happen when help arrived. Mac and J.R. would drop Connor and take off. Blake, well, Kendall hadn't figured out where he stood. His attitude wasn't as hard-core now as it was when they first met. These guys still had their guns and even though a hint of friendship may have occurred, Kendall knew enough not to overthink their actions or become too confident they'd let Haley and him go free.

He readjusted his pack on his back and examined the forest that lay before him. Without a worn trail to follow, his only option remained the same. Trek through the forest and make one. Each step tugged him forward. His weary legs ached. His knee rebelled some more but there was no time to stop.

A rush of wind caught him off guard as the familiar roar of fire steadily increased. Haley let go of his hand and clung to his shirt. Her eyes grew wide.

"Is that what I think it is?" Her voice shook.

Kendall gulped air. "Yes. Come on. The wind shifted and now the fire is rolling in our direction again."

"I thought we were safe right here." Blake ran up behind him. "Can it burn the already-burned areas?"

"Not likely, but look around. There's still plenty of foliage that didn't burn. Wind has a lot to do with the direction of the blaze, so don't ever assume you're safe until the fire is completely out." Kendall took Haley's hand and walked at a fast pace. Under the circumstances, it didn't matter if she needed to hold his hand or not. He had to know she was right behind him.

He glanced back at the others. J.R. and Mac lifted Connor up off the ground and jogged behind them. Blake stayed right behind Haley, who was behind Kendall. Everyone ran for their lives with what strength they had left.

Haley tumbled to the ground. Her hand jerked free from his. Kendall spun and assisted Blake in helping her to her feet.

"My ankle twisted in that hole, and I lost my balance." Haley slapped the dirt from her hands and reached for Kendall's. "I'm fine. No breaks, thank the Lord. Let's go."

"Are you sure?" Kendall shot a glance at Blake, then back at her. "Blake and I can carry you if you need us to."

"No, I'm okay. Let's go," Haley said.

No time to argue or examine her foot. Kendall took her hand in his again and walked at a fast pace. He couldn't see the fire yet, but he could hear it. The clearing was just ahead. He stayed focused on the open meadow. A few more steps. Just a few more steps. He could do this. Closer and closer until bright sunlight mixed with boiling smoke came into full view. The fire charged toward the meadow to the right of where they stood.

"Blake, take that Pulaski and start digging a fire line." Kendall pointed in front of the fire.

"No way." He tossed Kendall's Pulaski back to him. "You dig."

"I can help." Haley reached for the tool.

"Here." Kendall tossed his pack on the ground and pulled out his folding shovel. "Use this. I'll use the Pulaski." He retrieved his folding rake and tossed it to Blake, who caught the tool before it hit him. "You can do something if you want to survive."

Blake fell in line and began raking. The thrashing of his heart against Kendall's chest sent adrenaline shooting through his body like an electrical charge. Would they be able to withhold the massive fire coming their way? He dug into the ground with all the strength he could muster, but his efforts were futile compared with the massive fire raging toward them. Haley pushed the shovel into the earth with her foot and tossed the grass aside. Mac and J.R. stood close by still holding Connor.

Embers shot into the air and dropped on the ground around them. Flames shot up from the dried grass and ignited fallen leaves. Kendall grabbed Haley, causing her to drop the folding shovel. Didn't matter, he could get another one. Their lives were on the line.

"Run," Kendall said. "We've got to get past this blaze before we're pinned in." He focused on the only way out and the gap in the fire was closing in fast.

Haley let out a scream. "It's so close. How can it move so fast?"

Blake caught up to them. "I'd rather be in my jail cell."

Kendall quickly looked back to see where the others were. He stopped abruptly. J.R. and Mac had dropped Connor in the grass and were gaining ground behind them. "Blake, take Haley. I'm going back for Connor."

Kendall clenched his jaw. How could any human leave another to burn to death? Haley was almost a casualty until he rescued her. He wasn't about to leave Connor, regardless of his convict status.

Flames jumped at him like arms. The heat intensified. He rushed to Connor, who looked shocked that anyone cared to save him.

"You risked your life to come back for me?" Connor held his hand out for help up.

"Of course—firefighters never leave anyone behind." Kendall tugged Connor to his feet and draped Connor's arm around his shoulder. "Besides, it's ~~God~~ would want me to do, too. Every life has

The blaze ~~.~~

moaned, but he managed to flop ~~.~~ ~~.dall's~~ heels. Connor with long strides while hanging on to him. Perspiration rolled down Kendall's face and back.

"Almost there. Hang on." Kendall readjusted his grip on Connor. "We're going to make it."

Blake and Haley met them and helped him into the open meadow. They weren't out of danger yet.

The sound of helicopters overpowered the fire's roar. Kendall's breath hitched. Then a DH-6 300 Twin Otter plane came into view. Mac and J.R. started shooting at the helicopters. Kendall and Blake sat Connor down and the two of them ran toward the shooters. Kendall tackled Mac, knocking his pistol out of his hand. Blake tackled J.R. They rolled on the ground, fighting. Kendall jumped up ready to pounce on Mac again when Connor unexpectedly tossed his gun to him.

"I'm done," Connor said. "Take me back to prison."

Kendall scooped up Mac's weapon before Mac reached it and grabbed J.R.'s pistol. He stuck them in his waistband and held Connor's gun on the two men. "Give it up, guys. I can't let you hurt anyone else. This fire is on us and you're still only thinking of yourselves. Those are the smoke jumpers, risking their lives to save us."

Eight firefighters jumped from the plane and landed across the meadow in the distance. Kendall's insides shouted for joy. His eyes scrolled the forest line close to where the jumpers had landed and spotted his handcrew emerging from the s— the same area.

He lifted his ~~~~~~~~~~~~~ waved at them. "Hey! Over here." Such a jubilant moment.

He took Haley's hand as she stood beside him, staring. "We did it, Haley. We made it. Help has arrived." He looked back at the fire still coming toward them.

She let out a squeal, and jumped into his arms so fast he stumbled back and almost lost his footing. She squeezed, then pushed back.

The meadow came alive with sounds of chain saws and men yelling. An airplane flew over in the distance and released red spray into the flames.

"What is that?" Haley spun.

"Flame retardant to help put out the fire. Those guys with the chain saws are called sawyers because they fell trees." Kendall waved his arm again at his handcrew.

"Arggg!" Connor yelled, holding his leg. He turned to Kendall. "Thank you for coming after me. I'm going to look into this God stuff. I don't know anyone who would run back into a fire for somebody like me."

Mac and J.R. took off running toward the top of the hill. Connor sat on the ground holding his leg and moaning. Blake stood beside Haley and didn't move.

As the men reached the top of the hill, Rangers and police emerged from the opposite side. Mac and J.R. ran right into their hands. Police descended into the meadow, stood over Connor and radioed for a medic.

"Before I'm taken away, Haley, tell me how I can have faith like yours," Blake said.

"It's nothing difficult. I'm not perfect." Haley turned and faced her cousin. "I struggle with stuff all the time, just like everyone else. All you have to do is ask God to forgive you for all the things you've done wrong and ask the Lord to come into your heart. Simple as that."

Blake dropped to his knees in front of everyone and prayed as he wept. Kendall stilled and prayed his own prayer just to make sure he'd cleared things with God. Haley spoke up and prayed for Connor, Mac and J.R. to find a relationship with God, too.

Too bad Blake had to go back to prison with a possible extended sentence. His demeanor and attitude had shifted through their nightmare. Kendall evaluated his own attitude. All seemed well now that he'd cleared the air with God, so he guessed he was okay.

Blake surrendered to the police without incident and was escorted to a waiting helicopter that had landed on the side of the hill. Kendall rushed Haley to a separate chopper and watched her get buckled in her seat. He kissed her hand as the medic placed the oxygen mask over her nose and mouth.

"You handled yourself like a pro the past few days. If our paths cross again, maybe we can go out to that dinner we talked about." Kendall backed away from the helicopter and watched it disappear through the smoke-filled sky.

There was so much more he'd wanted to say to Haley.

Would he ever see her again?

Chapter Thirteen

Haley removed the oxygen mask long enough to gulp down some water. Her gaze remained on Kendall. He ran across the meadow toward his team until dark gray smoke blocked her view. He'd kissed her hand. That had to mean something. He'd said they should go to dinner. Her heart squeezed at the thought. Was she reading too much into his actions and words? Was it all a kind gesture on his part to keep her from giving up?

His fortitude and commitment to his job made a big impression on her. His honesty throughout their journey added to the sense that he was a man of integrity. He was a keeper. If only he felt the same about her. He'd distanced himself for a while during their harried episode, which raised doubts he wasn't interested in pursuing a relationship. He'd kissed her again during their joyous reunion after she'd been swept away in the river the second time.

The constant whop, whop, whop of the helicopter

bypassed the headset they put over her ears. In between clouds of smoke and occasional clear skies, they flew over the angry blaze consuming the forest. Such a huge, horrendous fire. If she hadn't survived herself, she'd never have believed anyone could. Without Kendall, she'd be among the fatalities. He'd saved her life and the lives of her cousin and the other escapees.

Thoughts of her rescue threatened tears. She was safe, and while Kendall continued to battle the blaze, the realization that these Forest Service firefighters were unbelievably fearless and persistent in battling such an overpowering force overwhelmed her. With death at life's door every time they engaged a wildfire, these men were to be commended for their faithful service. She couldn't imagine the stamina it took to do their jobs.

"Where are you taking me?" Haley stared at the magnitude of smoke filling the sky.

"To the hospital," the medic said.

"No, please, could you take me to where the firefighters receive first aid?" She stared out the window, doubting they'd allow it. "I need to speak with Kendall's superiors to let them know he is a well-trained, respectable man of integrity that takes his job seriously. He saved my life, I need to thank them in person for the excellent help of the Forest Service firefighter. Is that possible?" If only she could see Kendall one more time. She'd tell him her true feelings.

"They don't normally receive civilians, but you

would receive aid sooner if we take you back down to the medic tent. We'll radio down and see what they say." He nodded and spoke into the mic attached to his helmet.

She couldn't understand what he was saying because of the noise inside the chopper. Her body tilted to the right as the chopper turned, leveled and descended to the ground.

"They okayed your presence for a couple of hours. Said they'd like to meet you, too, then a truck will take you wherever you need to go."

"Thank you. I really appreciate you doing this for me." Excitement mounted.

The medic hopped out, and another opened her door. What a sight she must have been after four days in the forest with no shower, only dirt, mud and soot. They didn't seem to mind as they escorted her to the first aid tent, still sporting her oxygen mask.

"I need you to sign this release." The medic handed her a clipboard.

She signed the release form and handed it back. He left, and she sat on the edge of a cot. A tall man she estimated to be in his fifties stepped inside the tent.

"Hello, young lady. I'm Frank Davidson, fire medic. The captain will be here shortly to meet with you, as you requested." He sat on a rolling stool, scooted close to her and handed her a cold bottle of water. "I assume from all the radio chatter that you're Haley Gordon. Kendall told us about you over the radio a bit ago. From the looks of all those bruises, cuts and scrapes, you've had quite an ordeal."

"It was definitely an experience. If it weren't for Kendall, I wouldn't be here today."

He pushed the half sleeve up on her wounded arm. "What happened here? Looks like the near miss of a gunshot wound." His eyebrows lifted. He leaned back and eyed her.

She slumped her shoulders. "There was a fight and one of the escapee's guns went off. It hit my arm."

"Brave girl. Let's get you fixed up. When was the last time you had anything to eat or drink? Your blood pressure is a little low. Nothing a little fluid won't resolve." He reached into the drawer of a small portable cabinet and extracted tubing for an IV and a bag of fluid.

"Guess that's why I feel so drained."

"Dehydration will do strange things to the body," Mr. Davidson said. "Count your blessings that you made it out alive." He cleaned her wounds and applied antibiotic cream over her bullet wound, then wrapped a gauze bandage around her arm.

"Can't help but thank God after all that's happened." She bit back tears of relief. "I had to trust Him for protection and wisdom."

The medic inserted the IV needle and hung the solution bag on an IV pole. "You must be one tough lady to want to hang around here with that fire still blazing." He rolled his stool back.

"Kendall is the tough one. He kept his wits about him the entire time and saved all of us, despite the threats."

"What's this about Kendall?" A uniformed man stepped inside the tent. "I'm Captain Alex Hamilton. I understand you wanted to see me before you leave."

"Yes, sir. I'm Haley Gordon." She took in a deep breath. "I wanted to see you in person and commend you and the Blue Ridge Mountain Forest Service Firefighting Division for the amazing job you all do in the field, especially Kendall Simpson. He is, well, he's amazing. He taught me so much about fires while we were trying to escape, and he bragged about all his coworkers."

"Thank you, young lady. We take great pride in what we do, and Kendall is an asset to the team."

Haley told him about several of their encounters and how Kendall's wisdom kept them moving in the right direction and how he handled the escapees.

"Well, you rest up. We're all happy this ended well for everyone, and the escapees are on their way back to prison." Alex stepped toward the tent opening. "I need to get back to the command center. Take care, Haley."

The truck motor roared to life and what sounded like more vehicles pulled up. She sat back and studied her ragged fingernails. Not that they mattered that much right now. As soon as her IV finished, she'd be on her way.

A commotion outside the tent caught her attention. Curiosity got the best of her, so she slipped to the side of the tent's door and peeked out. A man and a woman rushed toward a firefighter getting out of a truck.

"Oh, Kendall." The woman's voice was filled with compassion.

Kendall?

Haley's heart fluttered. She was about to see him again, like she'd prayed. Did he know she was inside the tent?

The woman started crying and pulled Kendall into a hug. She wept on his shoulder, patting his back. Haley could only assume those were his parents. She eyed his dad, waiting for his response to his son.

"You're safe now. I was so worried about you with those dangerous escapees running free," his mom said through her tears. "We're so proud of you." She backed away and looked at his dad.

Haley held her breath. *Lord, please mend this relationship between father and son.*

His dad stepped forward and held out his hand for a handshake. "You've done a brave thing, son."

Kendall hesitated as his dad's hand hung in the air. Haley's shoulders began to tense.

Please, Lord.

Suddenly, Kendall threw his arms around his dad and embraced him. "I love you, Dad. I don't want any more tension between us. I miss our times together."

His dad reciprocated the embrace. He slapped him on the back and held on to his shoulder. "I'm proud of you, son. I was wrong to plan your life the way *I* wanted it. I didn't allow you to be the man *you* wanted to be. I love you, too, and I won't hassle you about the family business anymore. Can you ever forgive me?"

Tears of emotion flooded Haley's eyes. She knew she shouldn't be listening in on this personal family moment, but she was thrilled that God had answered her prayer.

Kendall touched his dad's shoulder. "There's nothing to forgive. You're my dad and you were looking out for me. I appreciate all you've done for me. It's good to be back."

"Now that we know you're okay, we'll go back home."

"I've got to finish up here before I can leave, but I'll see you in the morning after I get cleaned up and get some rest." Kendall waved goodbye as his parents headed back to their car, then drove away.

Haley rushed to the cot and sat down, biting her lip.

Kendall stepped inside the tent and stopped. She looked up. His eyes widened.

"What are you doing here?" His eyes lit up. "I thought you were long gone by now."

Her heart thudded. God had to have arranged this divine intervention. She hadn't expected to see Kendall so soon, but was thrilled for the opportunity to share her feelings with him.

"I… I needed to see you." She slipped off the cot still hooked up to the IV and took a step toward him. "I couldn't leave without thanking you for risking your life for mine."

He stepped closer to her. "I'd do it all over again if needed."

"That's not all." She hesitated. "I, uh, wanted you

to know that I really like you, and I don't know how you feel about it, but I've fallen in love with—"

He pulled her into his arms, pressed his lips to hers. She reciprocated the embrace.

Finally, a real kiss.

Chapter Fourteen

Eight months later

Haley could hardly wait for Kendall's arrival. She'd moved into an apartment in a small town closer to the mountains and closer to Kendall. The local dentist's office was looking for a dental assistant and she got the job. She figured it was partly because of her experience and partly because of all the publicity Kendall and she received after surviving the fire and helping authorities capture the escapees. Somehow the office felt they had more clout in the community because of her heroism. She stopped talking about it so everyone would quit asking her to repeat the story.

She'd never forget how nervous she was on her first date with Kendall. He was handsome as ever in his blue jeans and red pullover. His hair had a slight wave to it and one strand hung down on his forehead. A small addition to his good looks.

Their evening together started out with nervous

energy, but quickly switched over to a relaxed, peaceful outing. Kendall was quite the gentleman and kept the conversation going. He announced he had passed his test for the promotion he wanted and would continue his forestry firefighting education for further advancement. The excitement in his eyes confirmed how much he loved his job, and she loved it for him.

Haley glanced out of her front window. He wasn't due to arrive for another half hour. His mother invited them over for dinner in honor of Kendall's birthday. She'd said Haley didn't need to bring a gift. However, Haley had ordered the perfect present. It arrived a few days ago, and she was eager to see his face when he pulled it out of the gift bag. He'd never guess she'd bought him a new pair of men's adjustable sandals. His old ones were in a box in her closet. She couldn't bear to part with them. They held too many memories.

Kendall wheeled into a parking space in his black pickup. She stood at the window and watched as he bounced out and strode to her door. Before he knocked, she opened the door and received a kiss, just as she had every time they'd seen each other for the past eight months. Not that they didn't kiss in the first month. She'd set the boundaries to one kiss at the end of each date night until they knew each other better.

"Are you ready?" He stepped inside her doorway. "Looks like you were watching for me."

"How did you know?" She laughed. "I got ready earlier than expected. I just love your mom and dad and I'm looking forward to her delicious cooking." Haley tossed her crossover purse over her head, adjusted it by her side, grabbed the gift bag and walked out. He closed the door behind her.

Kendall opened the truck door for her. "There weren't supposed to be gifts."

"I know, but this one's special." She couldn't hold back her smile.

"If you say so." He closed her door and hopped around to the driver's side and got in. "Don't want to be late for my birthday dinner."

She met him midway across the seat when he leaned toward her for another quick kiss. She could do this forever. Old trust issues had faded in the forest, and he had continued to prove himself throughout the past few months. God had answered her prayers over and above what she'd asked. Life was never perfect, but with God as the head of their relationship, the two of them could resolve any situation as it arose.

They bounced over potholes along the wooded area where his parents lived. The beauty of summer foliage amazed her. His parents' yard was always in pristine condition, even the area where an old stump used to be. Kendall told her recently that he'd helped his dad take out the eyesore. Their first project together after reconciling their differences. She couldn't imagine the mountain of disappointment and hurt they had overcome.

Once he'd stopped in the paved driveway, Kendall hopped out and sprinted to open her door. Met with another brief peck on the lips, she and Kendall entered his parents' house. The sweet smell of freshly baked cake mixed with the aroma of pot roast met her nose. She set her purse and gift bag down on the sofa and went into the kitchen.

"Wow. This is country cooking at its finest." Haley hugged his mom and gave a side hug to his dad. "Thank you for inviting me."

"Oh, honey, we couldn't have eaten without you. I'm so glad you made it." His mom grabbed pot holders and pulled a large pan out of the oven. "You're just in time. Everything is ready, including the cake. Homemade chocolate icing, too. Kendall's favorite." Her eyes sparkled.

Kendall kissed his mom on the cheek and shook hands with his dad. "You know how to make me happy, Mom. Feed me and I'm good."

Everyone chuckled as they sat at the table, said the blessing and indulged in the delicious meal. His mom told stories of Kendall's childhood and all the birthday parties he had. She shared about how he'd tripped and had fallen into his birthday cake when he was sixteen.

Haley laughed and rubbed her stomach. "Oh, the food was amazing. I ate too much."

"We still have to sing and blow out the candles and eat cake." His mom's chair screeched across the floor as she jumped up to get the cake.

Sing? Haley bit her lip. Singing wasn't her forte.

"Really, Mom." Kendall placed his napkin on the

table. "I'll blow out the candles, but let's not sing. I'm twenty-eight, not six."

"I don't care how old you are, you're still my baby boy." She set the cake on the table with two lit candles in the center, the number two and the number eight. "Since he's too grown up for us to sing anymore, can we all just say 'happy birthday'?"

Everyone did as she requested, and he blew out the candles.

"I feel like a kid." He pulled the candles off and set them aside.

"Hold on." Haley jumped up and retrieved the gift bag. She handed it to Kendall. "Happy birthday."

His mom and dad sat quietly and watched the exchange. Kendall tossed one sheet of green tissue paper at a time on the floor until he reached in and pulled out his new sandals.

He burst out laughing. "Perfect. This is so perfect." He held them in the air. "Definitely brings back memories."

It registered with his parents what the memories were. His dad's shoulders shook as he chuckled, and his mom covered her mouth with her hand.

"Thank you for carrying sandals in your bag and being willing to sacrifice them to save my feet." Haley gave him a hug. "I owe you so much more. Thank you for saving my life. Happy birthday."

Kendall scooted his chair back and pulled her to her feet. He hugged her and kissed her on the cheek, right there in front of his parents. Haley had changed his life.

"Thank you for my sandals. You can wear them anytime you'd like." He chuckled.

His mom stood and insisted on cleaning the kitchen by herself. She rushed them out the back door while his dad shifted to the recliner in the living room with the TV remote.

Kendall escorted Haley outside to walk the meadow behind the house. The setting sun hung at the top of the trees and cast orange, red and yellow hues across the sky. Bluish lines of mountain ranges were visible in the distance. June temperatures gradually dropped into the seventies the more the sun disappeared behind the trees.

He held her hand as they strolled along the forest's edge. "I love the peace of being in the mountains. Don't get me wrong, I like the city when I have a reason to go."

"I never thought I'd live outside the city." Haley picked a wildflower and sniffed it. "After our horrific episode, one would think I'd never want to come back here. Even during all the danger, I found the mountains intriguing and beautiful. Guess that's why I moved closer."

Kendall stopped and faced her. "Oh. I thought you moved to be closer to me." He smiled at her and winked.

"Of course I did, but I couldn't tell you. We'd only just met." She batted her eyes at him. "So now you know. My secret's out."

He put his hand on her waist and pulled her close. "And I was shocked, to say the least, to see you sitting inside the medic's tent that day after being rescued from the fire."

"I was just as shocked that God had formulated a plan. He knew I wanted, no, I needed to see you and share my real feelings. Who knew you'd steal my heart in the midst of danger?"

"I could say 'ditto' to that."

He gave her a slow, lingering kiss before backing away and continuing their stroll back toward the house. "Do you have plans tomorrow?" He surmised she was free, and he had already made special plans for her. All he needed was confirmation.

"Saturday? Not really. I'm going to check on my parents, but otherwise I'm free all day." Haley squeezed his hand. "Dad's been doing so well after his heart surgery."

"Thought we'd go on a picnic. There's a scenic view I'd love to show you. It's a couple of miles up the mountain behind my house. The weather is only supposed to be in the low eighties."

Her smile always weakened his knees. She was jovial, fun-loving, and smart. How could he have found a jewel like her? Only God. Because of her, he discovered a genuine relationship with God and a peace that only comes from Him.

"I can't remember the last time I went on a picnic. That sounds amazing. Yes. What time?"

He released the breath he'd held. His plans were coming together. "Let's say I pick you up at ten in the morning. What time were you going to your parents' house?"

"Oh, Mom gets up as soon as the sun rises. Dad usually beats her to the kitchen and makes coffee. I'll be over there around seven, have breakfast with them and head home. Ten will give me plenty of time to be ready for our day."

The back door opened, and his mom stepped out onto the porch. "You kiddos best come in before the mosquitoes eat you alive."

"Coming, Mom." Kendall noted Haley smiling.

"She's so sweet. I just love her." Haley giggled. "She called us kids. Too funny."

They went inside and visited for a few minutes. Kendall thanked his mom for the birthday dinner. Haley hugged her and told his dad goodbye. Then Kendall drove her home with plans for the picnic rolling around in his head.

"You seem in deep thought." Haley turned her head toward him. "Care to share?"

Oops. He hadn't meant to be readable.

"Oh, the evening was extra special with you there. My parents have attached themselves to you." It was the truth. They loved her. He loved her. But he couldn't ruin the picnic, not now. He'd planned it all out.

She sat back and watched the road. "They are wonderful. I'm looking forward to our picnic. Who knew you could come up with such a genius idea?"

If you only knew. This is not about me. It's about you.

He walked her to her apartment door, kissed her and backed away. "I'll see you at ten."

"Looking forward to it." She closed the door.

He exhaled and shot a victory fist in the air. His plan was coming together. If all went well, by this time tomorrow, his dreams would come true. Her special gift sat on his dresser and he could hardly wait to give it to her.

Anticipation of their lunch date kept him restless through the night. He couldn't remember ever being this nervous. She loved him. He knew it and he loved her more than he ever thought possible.

Morning arrived none too soon. He hopped up at the break of dawn and grabbed his extra-large backpack loaded with preparations for lunch. Well, except for the food. He looped one arm through the open backs of two folding chairs, then grabbed the small round table with the other hand. The back door slammed behind him. He trekked up the mountain toward his designated spot. Glad he was in shape and could make it in record time. The ridge came into view and the sunrise still painted the sky.

He dropped everything on the ground and set up the folding table and chairs. He emptied his backpack containing a fitted tablecloth, napkins, two plates, two drinking glasses and silverware. Oh, in the side pocket was a flower vase.

His pulse beat overtime and sweat rolled down his back. She deserved this memorable moment, and he intended on surprising her with it.

Please let this be the surprise of a lifetime.

After setting up the dining table with a perfect view of miles of mountains, he roamed the area and picked wildflowers to fill the vase. Once everything was in order, he placed the empty backpack on his back and jogged home to shower before he picked her up.

He called his mom.

"Good morning. Is everything ready?" Kendall's voice cracked. His nerves were on edge.

His mom chuckled. "Yes, son. Everything's packed in my old picnic basket. Your dad will put it in your kitchen before you and Haley get back to your house."

"You're the best. Gotta go."

Kendall showered and hurried to the truck. He couldn't be late for this special occasion. He sped around curves, wiped perspiration from his brow and pulled into her apartment complex.

Before entering her door, he took a moment to calm himself down. Knowing her, she watched out the window. He put a smile on his face and walked toward her apartment. She stepped out wearing tennis shoes, ankle-length jeans and a sleeveless blouse. She'd pulled her hair up in a ponytail. He noticed her frosted pink lips.

"I'm ready." She smiled at him. "I've been ready. This is so exciting."

She slid across the truck seat. He leaned over and kissed her before shutting the passenger door. She couldn't be any more ready for this day than he. Kendall got in his seat and drove to his house. "You're going to be amazed at the view."

Her face brightened. "Great."

They walked through his house and out the back door. Kendall grabbed the picnic basket his dad had dropped off. He took her hand, and they trekked through the woods.

"I did not know your property went up this far." The light breeze tossed her floral perfume through the air and right into his nose.

Nice.

They emerged from the woods to the small area where the open-air dining table sat in place with the chairs, dishes and flowers.

Her jaw dropped. "Kendall, what is this?" She spun and looked every direction, then stopped at the magnificent mountain view. "Wow. I'm overwhelmed. You are amazing. Look at this setup. When did you ever have time? The view is indescribable."

He set the picnic basket on the table and stepped beside her. "I wanted today to be special, like you." He dropped to one knee a safe distance from the cliff and opened the small white box, exposing a one-carat marquise-cut diamond.

"Kendall?" Her hand covered her mouth and her eyes widened.

"Haley Gordon, I've loved you from the moment our eyes met and my love for you has intensified each day since. Will you marry me?"

Happy tears ran down her cheeks. She let out a squeal and jumped into his arms.

"Yes. Yes. I thought you'd never ask."

He planted his lips on hers. The kiss he'd only

dreamed would come after she said yes. They parted. He took her hand and slid the ring on her finger.

He locked eyes with her. "I'll love you always and forever."

"Me, too." She fell into his arms again and buried her head against his chest. "You are my true hero. I love you."

"Shall we eat? Mom made your favorite fried chicken, and she even made us a miniature wedding cake."

"You've got to be kidding. Your parents had a part in this?"

He pulled the chair out for her, and he sat on the opposite side. "Yes. They knew last night. Mom had already made the cake."

"Kendall Simpson. You amaze me. I can't believe you did all this for me."

"You're worth every bit. I would move mountains for you."

* * * * *